A DARKER PATH

C. G. COOPER

"A DARKER PATH"

Book 15 of the Corps Justice Series

By C. G. Cooper

A portion of all profits from the sale of my novels goes to fund OPERATION C4, our nonprofit initiative serving young military officers. For more information visit OperationC4.com.

Want to stay in the loop?
Sign Up to be the FIRST to learn about new releases.
Plus get newsletter only bonus content for FREE.
Visit cg-cooper.com for details.

Join my private reader group at TeamCGCooper.com.

CHAPTER ONE

Beating heart.

Twice, three times as fast as it should've been.

The boy crouched in a dingy alcove, panting as quietly as he could.

His curiosity had finally come back to bite him. His dead mother had often told him not to go poking about. "The neighborhood boys don't like it," she'd said.

But he never listened. Left to himself, Pindip ran the streets with his friends, barely recognizing the danger all around. It was only natural. A child turned part animal. Curious to a fault.

Now he felt it, as keen as a blade pressed to his throat. *Danger*.

He swallowed once. Then again. He was thirsty.

Shouting. Scuffles and jostling from the far end of the alley.

Shadows parted. There they were. Five teenagers. Pushing twenty and all swagger, as if they'd been plucked by the emperor himself for their task. Untouchable.

Mother was right, he thought. *I'm afraid and stupid.*

Quiet as a mouse.

The older boys came closer, clanging sticks along the dented trashcans, sending rodents skittering away to safety.

"Come out, little rat," one of the young punks said.

"Yes, come and play, little rat!" another said.

Why had he been so stupid? To spy on the ring of thugs seemed like such a fun thing to do at the time. Something he did whenever he skipped school. But he'd slipped and shown himself with the clang of a junk metal hubcap. It would've been bad enough if they'd heard him and he'd run. But they'd seen him.

And of all the gangs in the city, he had to pick this one. They were said to have ties with terrorists. New recruits ready to prove themselves. Pindip hadn't believed the whispers, but what he'd seen made him a believer.

So much blood. So much death. A house of horrors. The experienced eyes of the orphan knew evil when it lay before him. At six, he already knew the truth: Evil, like love, was behavior.

"Come, little rat," they called over and over.

CRASH.

Pindip thought they'd thrown a can in his direction. But he felt no debris scatter at his feet. He cautioned a peek around the wood planks he hid behind. The punks had turned the other way.

"Go away," their leader said, the one who'd slashed the throat of the man in the house.

Pindip leaned further. There was a man at the end of the alley bathed in backlight. The boy couldn't see the man's face.

"Leave the boy alone," the man said in English.

Pindip knew English. He'd learned it from watching American movies, and he'd met a real American once, a soldier of some sort. The man had given him chocolate, not like the kind Pindip often stole from the local market. This was sweet and filled his mouth with warmth, like a vacation far away.

"Go away," the gang leader said, holding a machete in the air to scare the stranger away.

"Not gonna happen, kid."

The teens looked from one to another. Pindip felt their indecision. They were crazy not to run. He felt like he should run—

No. He wanted to see. There was that nagging curiosity again.

"We hurt you," the leader said, trying to sound tough in his broken English.

"We *will* hurt you," said the stranger. "The simple future tense. You should learn it if you're going to get anywhere in life."

Pindip knew better. He heard the fear, could almost feel it like the tickle of cold that ushered in the deep nights of winter. Living on the streets gave him unique insight into the human psyche. It helped him stay alive.

Now he felt something else entirely. Something strange, menacing, and yet pulling.

Pindip leaned in farther, no longer caring if the older boys saw him. They were entranced by the stranger.

"Go!" yelled the one with the machete. "Ten second!"

"*Seconds*," corrected the stranger.

"Five second!"

"End of the road then, boys," the man said.

Confusion. They didn't know what that meant. Pindip did. He'd heard it in a movie.

Whispers from the gang. Then, on cue, they rushed forward.

The leader hung back, letting his charges move first.

The first teen came close. The man didn't move until the last possible moment.

And then his arm came through in a high arc. Pindip saw it now, something in the man's grasp.

The thin rod came crashing down onto the rushing teens head.

Crack and splat.

The teen crumpled. Pindip knew he was dead. He'd seen an old man killed in such a way, but that had been with a stout club wielded by a jungle rebel. This man had done it with a thin metal rod no longer or wider than Pindip's own arm.

The sudden death of their compatriot gave the others pause. But not for long.

The leader called out two names, and two more attackers flew at the man at the end of the alley.

Parry. Strike. Parry. Strike.

The man barely moved. He dispatched the two like he was cutting down stalks of sugar cane.

"Who's next?"

The leader glanced fearfully at his final charges. Both shook their heads. As one, they dropped their weapons, at least that's what they showed the man. But Pindip saw the leader's hand drop to the small of his back.

"Look out!" Pindip cried.

The gun came out of the leader's waistband. It was the same weapon he'd used to rob the woman on the corner who'd sometimes give Pindip a bite of breakfast when he was too hungry to steal. It was the same gun the leader had used to harass Pindip's neighbor, a poor cripple who waved his arms to Broadway show tunes for scraps of cash on the street. And finally, this morning, Pindip had watched while this same leather-faced leader gunned down three women, prostitutes probably, right there in that bloody shanty.

The squat black weapon swung around, for a second blotting out the pinpoint of late afternoon sun. The muscular arm moved it to the man's chest.

Pindip wanted to scream, but there was no time to do so as the weapon was leveled.

The stranger stood glued to the spot, feet spread shoulder width apart. He looked like an American cowboy. Pindip had seen plenty of them on television.

He moved now, as swiftly as he had with the baton. Only this time, he matched his opponent with a gun. A *bigger* gun.

The pistol came out with the ease of a master, fast and precise.

Two shots.

The hoodlum's weapon clattered to the ground.

"I told you to leave the boy alone," the man said.

"I go!" the last teen said, raising his arms like he was trying to touch the clouds.

The man took one step closer, then another. He nudged the leader with a boot.

"I'll never understand it," the man said, shaking his head. "All the potential in the world, and you choose to harass a neighborhood, chase a little boy." Another slow shake of the head.

"I go!" the teen said again, his voice laced with fear.

The man turned his gaze down the length of the alleyway. "You okay, kid?"

"Yes," Pindip said, trying to sound sure of himself.

"Thanks for the warning."

Pindip nodded.

The man turned to the last teen standing.

"And you. What to do with you?"

"I go!"

"*Will* go." He nodded to the distance.

The teen hesitated.

"I said go. Shoo."

The boy took off, bound for freedom.

Freedom never came.

Like the cowboys of the Wild West, the man shifted and fired from his hip. One. Two. Three. Four. Five. Six.

The would-be thug went down, and the man exchanged his empty magazine for another.

"Come here, kid," he said as he stuffed the weapon in his pocket.

Pindip froze.

"It's okay. I'm not gonna hurt you, I promise."

This from a man who just told a teen to go and then shot him anyway.

But there was something in the man's demeanor, his absolute calm. Like a tiger who would ravage prey but protect its kin.

Pindip took two tentative steps forward, his naked feet splashing in the grimy water of the alley floor.

"Come on," the man said with a sing-song tone.

Something propelled the boy toward the stranger.

"You got a place to live?"

Pindip shook his head.

"Any family?"

Again, the shake.

The man bent down to look the boy straight in the eyes. They were indeed a tiger's eyes, searching, knowing, cunning.

"Me neither, kid. Tell you what, there's a village a few minutes south with a white church. You know it?"

"Saint Ignatius," Pindip said in his best American English.

"That's right. You go there and you give the priest this." The man handed Pindip a white business card. There was nothing on the card except a border in black.

The boy looked up at the man unable to contain the question. "What it say?"

The man chuckled. "What *does* it say. And it's not what it says, it's what it doesn't. Give it to the priest. He owes me a few favors."

Pindip's curiosity bubbled forth again. "Who are you?"

"No one you need to think about, kid. Just remember, keep your nose clean. I'll be checking up on you."

The man turned to leave. "My name is Pindip."

The man paused and at first didn't turn. When he did, there was something else in his gaze. Compassion?

He bent down again and extended his hand. "Nice to meet you, Pindip. My name's Matthew, but don't tell anyone."

Pindip shook Matthew's strong hand. He was not a large man, not like the wrestlers in the village, but his hand bore the surety of two such men. Pindip knew such things.

The man rose, tousled Pindip's hair, and then stepped out into the light.

It wasn't the last time the orphan would see the strange man – his guardian angel.

CHAPTER TWO

"How do you feel?"

"Good."

"Can you give me more than *good?*"

Cal Stokes stretched an arm across his chest. The morning's workout was going to leave a mark.

"I'm *better*, Doc."

Dr. Alvin Higgins, lead interrogator and psychological pro of The Jefferson Group, peered over his glasses at the younger man. Higgins looked the part of the Ivy League shrink −studious eyes, elbow patches, and pipe sitting on the table next to his chair.

Stokes was the complete opposite. Where Higgins was round and doughy around the middle, Stokes was still all lean Marine, although he'd put on a considerable amount of muscle in the preceding weeks.

"You know I'm not trying to pry, Calvin." Higgins was the only man in the world who could get away with calling the *de facto* leader of TJG "Calvin". "You went through quite an ordeal."

"I know, Doc. And I promise, you'd be the first one I'd come to if I had a problem."

And he wasn't lying. Higgins was family, plain and simple. Not only did he have a world-class knack for cracking the worst terrorists on the planet, Higgins was a decent man, a friend who acted more like an uncle, someone who cared more than the majority of his head case peers.

Higgins looked down at Cal's file, even though the Marine knew he'd pretty much committed it to memory.

"Master Sergeant Trent says your physical recovery is complete. So, no surprises there."

"That's a relief. I'm tired of Top twisting me into a pretzel."

Higgins chuckled.

Marine MSgt Willie Trent was nearly seven feet in height with an NFL linebacker's physique. If Trent gave his approval, it meant Cal was ready to jump from airplanes.

"And Daniel seems to think your skills have improved. Tell me about that."

"Briggs said that?"

"He did."

"Well, he's right. My reflexes are tight, sharper. I can move faster, run longer."

Higgins tapped his chin once. "It's not uncommon to see that in a man in your profession. Add to that your father's proclivity for excellence, and what you see in the mirror each morning is the new and improved Calvin Stokes, Jr."

Cal nodded, digesting what he'd already suspected.

"You've made it through your ordeal and have come out stronger on the other side," Higgins added, making a note in the file. "I suspect you're ready to go operational?"

This time Cal's nod was less emphatic, almost automatic. The ever-astute Higgins didn't miss the move.

"You have reservations."

"Not reservations, Doc, just... I don't know. I guess I want to make sure I'm one hundred percent ready."

By "ordeal" Higgins was referring to Cal's cold mountain

incarceration months before. Over thirty days with no food, licking moisture off the walls to survive. They'd found him, emaciated, hallucinating – a changed man in more ways than one.

"You've made it over the spine of the roof, Calvin. You've dealt with the pain. You've rehabilitated your mind and body. You're ready."

Another half-hearted nod. "I know. It's just that... I don't..."

"You don't want to let the team down."

Cal looked up at his doctor, his friend. The Marine was no shrinking violet, but his time under the mountain in Wyoming had opened up a door that he couldn't seem to close.

"I don't doubt my skills. Really, I don't. But if there's even the chance that I could..."

"You won't. Even if you do, it's part of being human. Step into the sunlight, Marine. You made it back through hard work and determination. You deserve it."

Cal nodded, more confident this time. He clenched his fist and then flexed his forearm. It felt good to be back. And he liked the perks of being the new and improved Cal Stokes.

The two men stood, shook hands, and parted.

All the while Cal couldn't help but wonder if he'd been returned to the world too soon.

———

"WHAT DID HE SAY? Do we need to drive you to the loony bin?" Willy Trent exclaimed with clapping hands when Cal emerged from his final evaluation.

Cal grinned. "Only if you're coming with me, you lumbering beast."

Top stepped over and crushed Cal in a bear hug. There'd been more of those than ever since Cal's rescue. The warriors of TJG weren't huggers unless it was a special occasion.

"Can you put me down, Top?"

"Yeah, put him down so I can hug him too!" Gaucho, the shortest of TJG's warriors, a burly Hispanic with a dual braided beard, rushed over and received Cal in open arms.

"Jeez, you'd think I just rose from the dead or something," Cal groaned.

"You did, you dumb grunt," Top said. "And look at you now, Lazarus. Good as new. Better even."

"Like a Hollywood pretty boy," said Gaucho.

"Poster boy for the zombie apocalypse."

Top and Gaucho lent their comedic talent to the serious business conducted from TJG's Charlottesville headquarters. Cal couldn't help but laugh. Macabre humor was a Marine's lollipop.

Daniel Briggs, Marine sniper and resident warrior monk, stood to the side, watching the congratulations. His eyes met Cal's.

Cal knew that Daniel understood. While they'd all been through some type of hardship in their respective distinguished careers, Daniel, more than the others, knew what rock bottom meant, what it felt like when your soul scraped the crust of the world, all road rash and bleeding.

"What, no hug from Snake Eyes?" Cal asked innocently.

Daniel shook his head, smiling. "I'll leave that to the dynamic duo over there."

Top wrapped a tree trunk arm around Cal. "Okay, ladies. I think our boy's release from rehab deserves a drink at the bar. I'm buyin'."

THE NEXT MORNING came too soon. Cal's head throbbed, despite only having a single beer the night before. He grabbed the bottle of water from the nightstand and pounded the entire thing.

The clock next to the bed said 5:15am. He'd slept in.

Five minutes later, PT gear on and another bottle of water rushing through his body, he hustled out the door. When he arrived at the steps of the Rotunda at the University of Virginia, Daniel was waiting.

"Sorry I'm late," Cal said, hurrying to get some quick stretches in before their run. He had high hopes of beating the sniper for the first time. A leisurely jog through Grounds, what UVA students called their campus, followed by a meaty hill workout on O-Hill.

"You ready?" Daniel asked.

"Ready to beat you? Yep. I've got your number this time, Marine."

The thin smile from his friend did little to dispel Cal's confidence.

"Lead the way."

AN HOUR AND A HALF LATER, as Cal sprinted to the finish, Briggs was waiting for him.

"I thought I had you on the second circuit," Cal huffed.

Daniel's blond hair was lathered in sweat, but his countenance didn't match how Cal felt – ready to drop to the ground in a heap.

"Maybe next time. You've never been faster."

Cal started his post-run stretch routine. "You don't have to coddle me, you know."

"Have I ever coddled you?"

Cal smirked and gave his friend the finger.

"Keep that up and the hugs and coddling stop," Briggs deadpanned.

Two fingers this time.

Two Bodos cinnamon raisin bagels with ham, egg and cheese later, Cal felt like himself again.

"Doc says I'm ready."

"You already knew that," Daniel said, polishing off his orange juice.

"Yeah. I guess I did."

Daniel put the cup down. "You don't feel ready?"

"You've seen me, haven't you? I've never been better on the range. Everything about me is in top gear, despite not trouncing you on the run. I *will* beat you one day. You know that, right?"

Daniel shrugged. "What is it then? Something you talked to Higgins about?"

"You know how he is. Half the time I feel like he's speaking in riddles."

"Doesn't sound like the Doc Higgins I know."

Cal pushed his tray away. "I'm ready," he said, more emphatically this time.

"Good."

"So that's it."

"Unless you want to tell me more."

The gung-ho Marine in Cal was ready to rush enemy fortresses. It was the nagging sense of something incomplete that kept Cal in check. He'd never had so much time to think. He was a man of action, quick to pull the trigger when the timing was right. In fact, since coming home, his reaction time and decision-making ability felt heightened, fully weighing in his mind.

"You're right. You're all right. I need to get back to work. No more pussyfooting around."

Daniel tossed his cup in the trash and headed for the street. "Good, because Wilcox is waiting."

CHAPTER THREE

Matthew Wilcox placed the last pack of dried goods in St. Ignatius's humble pantry.

"Thank you," said Father Francis. "You have no idea how much you've helped."

"Not a problem, Padre. I just want to make sure the kids have food in their bellies."

"They will, thanks to you."

"Good." He rubbed his hands together. "And how's Pindip getting along? Settling in?"

The Filipino priest smiled. "It took time, but yes, our Pindip is quite the character. He asks about you."

"Oh?"

"He calls you his guardian angel."

"That's a first."

The priest smiled. It was all he could think of by way of response. He was used to treading lightly around the strange man with the American accent. He couldn't shake the feeling that beneath the good deeds being done for the church was a writhing snake waiting to strike.

"Well, that's it for today's grocery trip," Wilcox said, wiping a sleeve across his sweaty brow. "I'll be back in a month or so. Anything you need?"

Father Francis moistened his lips. He didn't want to ask, but he did. "The toilets."

"What about them? They need repairing?"

"Sometimes they work. Sometimes not."

"I thought the plumber took care of it." There was an edge to Wilcox's tone now.

The priest hesitated, not wanting to press the point. "It will be fine. We will fix it."

"No. I'll take care of it. Same plumber?"

The priest nodded sheepishly.

AN HOUR LATER, Wilcox returned with the plumber in tow.

The younger man went straight back to work while the plumber, his face pallid in panic, asked the priest exactly which toilets needed repairs. The priest told him. There were never any problems with the plumbing again.

CHAPTER FOUR

Come hell or high water, I'm doing this.

Cal rolled over in his bed, tousling the sheets to the floor.

Dammit.

When he bent over the side to retrieve the lost sheets, he caught sight of the picture on the bedside. He and Diane Mayer. His ex. The woman who could've been his wife.

Frozen in place, Cal studied her smiling face. The picture was taken in Seaside, Florida, one of their favorite places to go on the rare occasions the pair shared time off work.

While Cal's profession kept him busy traveling the world, saving its inhabitants from the deeds of the tyrannical few, Diane was ensconced in the world of Naval Intelligence.

He always used to tease her about that.

"Naval Intelligence? And I thought the idea of Marine Intel was absurd."

It was an old joke, and one she'd rolled her eyes at every time.

He sighed away the past. He'd ended the relationship. His fault. Not hers. She was as perfect a human being as he'd ever met. He couldn't tarnish that.

He picked up the framed image, opened the drawer, and slid the memory inside, closing the drawer gently.

Much like his life, he filed it away, far from the light of day.

*Ditch the dark thought*s, he thought, casting any idea of going back to sleep far into the future.

CAL ATTENDED to a slew of new emails, some from potential legitimate clients for The Jefferson Group, a couple from internal sources, detailing possible black ops, and finally a company-wide email from Neil Patel. Neil was the brains of TJG. Tech genius. Computer nerd. Indian ladies' man. He was another best friend, someone Cal had known since attending the University of Virginia.

The email was to the point:

Whoever keeps hiding my mouse, can you please grow up.
   Love, Neil.

Ah, the good times. TJG was equal parts serious outfit and increasingly a boys' club.

Cal was about to send a snarky reply when another email dinged in.

Unknown sender.

Probably spam.

He thought about just pressing delete. Long day ahead. No need to give the spammers the satisfaction of tracking that he's actually opened the email.

But he didn't ignore it. He opened it.

Hi, Cal. Long time no see.

Your pal,
Matthew.

Cal's skin prickled. He read the short message again. And once more.

Your pal, Matthew.

Matthew Wilcox was no friend of Cal or his TJG brethren. It had been Wilcox who had locked Cal away, left him to die. It was Wilcox who left the file. That damned file...

Righting himself, Cal forwarded the message to Neil, asking for tracking data, although he doubted Wilcox would make it that easy. He'd made quite a name for himself not only amongst The Jefferson Group, but in the public domain as well. He'd killed a shady Russian ambassador, two corrupt Wall Street tycoons, and an African despot who'd spent the last twenty years terrorizing his people.

Wilcox was building a reputation. Social media lurkers painted him as a caricature modern myth hero. A Jesse James for the historically ignorant. To them, Wilcox was a detergent cleansing society of its undesirables. As far as Cal was concerned, they were more or less correct on this point; every person Wilcox had killed in plain sight had deserved it. They were crooks, psychopaths, murderers. No one had mourned their passing.

But it was the way he did it that kept Cal and his team searching the globe. It was months since the first video of Wilcox, or who they'd presumed was Wilcox, killing the Russian on live television. A spectacle, yes. But the worst part was that somehow, inexplicably, the man's face on camera had been the face of Cal Stokes, leader of The Jefferson Group.

They'd run facial analyses then and on the subsequent scenes. It was a perfect match for Cal's likeness. Neil was able to fudge the details by hacking into networks, but the damage was done. Cal's face became a known quantity. From fuzzy black and white to full high definition.

Another email hit Cal's inbox. Unknown Sender.

It's time to meet. Are you ready?
    Your buddy,
    Matthew.

Cal shut his eyes tight. If only he could reach through the computer and strangle the bastard. He shut his laptop instead, having learned long ago what damage an errant pissed-off email could do.

It was time to talk to the team.

NOBODY SPOKE as Cal clicked from one email to the next.

"Funny guy, right?" Cal said, looking at the assembled team.

"He's trolling you," Gaucho said.

"Nothing on my end," Neil said, forever clacking away on one of his various computer stations situated inside the War Room.

"Maybe he'll send another message," Top said.

As if on cue, another email dinged in. Cal opened it.

Your call. Time's a tickin'.
    Forever yours,
    Matthew.

"I'm writing back."

As the others watched, Cal typed a quick reply.

Okay. When and where?

They waited, the only sound in the room was Neil typing and clicking. The reply came in under a minute.

Not so fast. I'm not some cheap date. There are things to discuss.
    MW

"This guy," Cal said, typing his reply.

Fine. What?

They waited. And waited. No reply.

The next sound in the room was the buzzing and dinging of every cell phone in the room.

They pulled the phones out of pockets, off desks.

Cal looked down at his phone.

One single image sent via text.

Cal clicked.

There, laying on probably some faraway couch was a mask, as realistic as if someone had peeled off their face and put it down where they'd just been sitting.

It was a face every person in the room knew. It was one of them. Everyone looked from their phone to the face in question.

Daniel Briggs stared back at them with a look of confused curiosity.

CHAPTER FIVE

Daniel walked alongside Cal, mulling.

"What?" Cal asked.

"You can't go."

"Why not?"

"You know why."

"Because it's dangerous?"

Daniel didn't answer. The sniper had a way of looking deep into Cal's subconscious. He'd never seen it, but he bet Briggs could give Higgins a run for his money in the interrogation game.

"I have to go," Cal said.

"You keep saying that."

Cal didn't want to explain. He was tired of explaining.

The truth was that he felt awful, but it was a sensation without a locus. Something deep inside that kept squirming, needing to be let out. It was what he might have to do to let it out that gave him pause.

"At least let us track you," Daniel said, his quiet persistence ever pushing.

"You know he'll think of that. You saw how he pinged all our phones. He's got us. I need to go alone."

They walked on for a few steps, each lost in silent contemplation.

Cal knew his friends would work to keep tabs on him, and that was fine. As long as he didn't know the details. He'd put them in enough danger.

"I never got to say thanks," Cal said.

"For what?"

"For looking when maybe you should've stopped."

It was Daniel who'd pushed the others to keep up the day and night slog through the snowy mountain landscape. It was Daniel who'd made the final discovery. And it was Daniel's face that Cal had seen upon being rescued.

"You would've done the same for me."

Cal nodded. No need to rehash. He *would* have done the same thing. That's what brothers did for one another. All joking aside, they were family, plain and simple.

"At least take Liberty with you. Wilcox can't keep you from taking her."

He smiled at the thought of taking his German Shorthaired Pointer along for the adventure, as the beautiful girl had become the unofficial mascot of the TJG gang. "I don't know."

"Take her. She'll watch over you."

Cal looked over at Daniel.

"What have you been teaching her now?"

Daniel shrugged. "She's a quick learner. She'll take care of you."

Cal hadn't lifted a finger to train the dog. It was Daniel who'd taken on that burden like so many others. Liberty should've been Travis's dog. Travis Haden. Navy SEAL. Former Chief of Staff to the president. Travis Haden. Cal's cousin.

Travis Haden. Dead.

How many more would there be?

Cal's parents. Cal's fiancé. Cal's friends.

Death stalked him like a bitch. When would it stop?

That's why he had to go. The mask with Daniel's face on it was a warning.

Come or I dress up as your buddy, the almost Medal of Honor recipient.

Cal shook the plunging thoughts away. If there was one thing he'd walked away from that cold mountain with, it was a keener sense of his emotions. He still wasn't sure how that fit in. He was still learning how to deal with the flood. Better to put up a dam and let it be.

"I'll take Liberty. At the very least, she'll be good company."

WILCOX SENT his next instruction later that day.

Get to LaGuardia.

Two guesses followed: 1) Wilcox was in New York. 2) Cal was going to Europe.

Perhaps Wilcox was working with the Chinese.

Cal let the others guess. This was Wilcox's game. It was foolish to think they could thwart the man's plans with mere speculation.

And as he watched his team bat pie-in-the-sky plans back and forth, Cal felt himself drift. Something pulled him. Adventure? Danger? A final reckoning?

He put a hand on Liberty's chocolate coat, stroking the fine animal as she lay her head in his lap, looking up at him with those expectant eyes.

"What do you say, girl? Are you ready for an adventure?"

The only response from Liberty was a slow wag of her cropped tail.

CHAPTER SIX

The flight to LaGuardia was uneventful. It helped to have a private Gulfstream at your disposal.

Cal gathered his things, along with a pack Daniel had sent for Liberty – food and assorted outdoor gear. Always the Boy Scout, that Briggs.

"We've got a guy in a black trench coat waiting in the receiving area," the pilot announced over his shoulder as they taxied to the private terminal.

Cal rose from his seat and stepped into the cockpit. Nothing about the man in the coat sparked recognition. Not that he would've known if it was Wilcox. They had old pictures of the criminal, but nothing to indicate what he looked like now.

Try to ID a chameleon.

The plane finished taxiing and Cal waited for the engines to die down.

"You sure you don't need anything else?" the pilot asked.

Cal knew what he was getting at. Weapons.

"I've got Liberty. What else do I need?"

The pilot's dubious look said it all: *"You're diving into the lion's den with nothing but a dog barely out of her puppy stage?"*

"Well, take care then," he said instead, offering his hand.

"Thanks. Hopefully I'll see you soon."

THE MAN in black hadn't said a word. He'd led Cal and Liberty to a stretch limo. He hadn't even offered to take the bags. Smart move.

Cal settled in as best as he could while Liberty stood with two paws on the seat, one always touching Cal as she gazed out the window, issuing the occasional low woof at the scene unfolding outside.

He'd expected a drive into the city. Nope.

They did a pass through the Greek labyrinth that is LaGuardia's main terminal, around an industrial section of the airport, and parked near a tiny building that looked like a tool shed.

The driver pointed to it and said, "In there."

"That's it?" Cal felt his blood pressure rising – that uptick before the clang.

The driver didn't answer. The doors unlocked. The driver sat in silence.

"Thanks for the scintillating conversation. Catch you on the return trip. Maybe you can give me a play-by-play of the city."

Still no response. Just a paid lackey, bored and blank-faced.

Liberty leapt from the vehicle first, approaching the tool shed like she was stalking a herd of buffalo, tail cocked at forty-five degrees.

Cal let her do her thing, coming close to the building only after she'd sniffed and prodded. She was no bomb-sniffer, but she had a sixth sense. Not unlike Daniel Briggs.

"What do you think, girl? Should we go in?"

Liberty didn't look up. She didn't twitch a muscle. Her focus was glued to the hut.

"Alright then." Cal reached out and grabbed the rusted handle. It was cold to the touch, the sweeping wind accentuating that feeling.

It was a tool shed alright. But one that had undergone ten rounds of spring cleaning. Every tool had a place on a rack, in a bin, or on a peg board. Tidy. Neat. Aligned.

Liberty was the first in, sniffing furiously. Cal watched, gazing around the small space that was no bigger than his living room. When Liberty had made a pass and started in on another, Cal stepped in further.

"What do you think, pup? Anything interesting?"

The roar of engine outside was his only answer. The car was leaving.

"Okay, Wilcox, where to now?" Cal wondered aloud.

"I thought you'd never ask," came the crystal-clear voice. It was piped into the shed by some electronic means, yet was so clear that Cal, if he didn't know any better, would have thought Wilcox had somehow figured out how to be invisible. "Sorry to scare you, pal o' mine. Figured it was best this way."

Liberty was glued to Cal's side now, shivering even. Cal reached a hand down and stroked her smooth coat. "Easy."

"I don't remember saying you could bring your dog."

"You didn't say I couldn't. You said come alone. I assumed that meant *sans* human companionship."

Silence.

Then came the low chuckle. Cal could imagine Wilcox's thin smile.

"You win," Wilcox said. "The dog should make things interesting."

The way he said "interesting" made Cal think he shouldn't have brought Liberty.

"What's next, Wilcox? Is this the next test?"

"Why? Did you study?" Again, the low laugh.

"Cut the crap. What next?"

"Patience, Marine. You really should learn how to relax. Speaking of relaxed, how are you with tight spaces?"

"Just fine."

"And water? Still wake up thirsty?"

Cal gritted his teeth. "What do you want, Wilcox?"

"Wilcox? No. Too formal. You're not in the Marines anymore. Call me Matthew. I'd like for us to be friends."

Cal bit his tongue before he could blurt his spite-filled reply. "Fine, *Matthew*. What now?"

"I thought we'd get a little sun. I'm sure you'd rather hit the beach than ski the frozen tundra. What do you say?"

"This is your game."

Now Wilcox's voice went hard, cold even. "This is no game, Cal. This is life. If you're not going to take this seriously, I'll just call in the cavalry, kill you, then move on to your friends in Charlottesville. Is that what you want?"

Liberty issued a low growl that reverberated within the metal walls of the enclosure.

Again came the chuckle. "I guess the pooch understands. Okay then. Now that we're on the same page, why don't we get the show on the road. There's a car behind the building you're standing in. Keys are in the ignition and a map is on the passenger seat. Follow the directions and I'll see you soon. And try not to get dog hair all over everything, will you? I'm paying for this stuff."

"Is there a timeline?" Cal asked.

No answer.

Cal and Liberty exited the building and made their way to the vehicle, a nondescript hunter green SUV with Connecticut plates. As promised, the keys were in the ignition, and a map was on the seat next to him. Liberty was in the back, front paws planted on the middle console. Eyes straight ahead.

"Well, girl, you ready for the next leg of our adventure?" He scratched her behind the ears. The dog, ever vigilant, stood statue stiff.

CHAPTER SEVEN

The drive led into the city where Cal wound through the stop-and-go traffic, expecting surprises at every turn. There was no name on the circled destination on the map, nor was Cal familiar enough with Manhattan to know where he was headed.

Around Central Park they drove, Liberty's gaze shifting at the sight of horse-drawn carriages and joggers passing by. Cal knew his geography enough to know that they were headed to the Upper East side, money town.

A couple more turns and they arrived at their destination, a tall brick building with a low green awning out front and a doorman already at the curb.

He opened the door for Cal.

"Mr. Stokes?"

"That's me."

"Can I take your bags, sir?"

"I think I can handle them."

Cal stepped out with Liberty quick on his heels.

"Do you have a leash, sir?" the doorman asked.

"Nope."

The doorman looked like he was going to lecture Cal on New York City leash laws but he didn't.

"If you'll follow me please, sir," he said impatiently.

They brushed past the main elevator, down a back hall to a private service elevator. Up they went, faster than any elevator Cal had ever been in. The floors dinged by, one per second. They stopped at 20.

"If you'll follow me please, sir."

Liberty was close at hand, eyes pegged ahead.

There was a metal door up ahead. Cal could hear the drone of engines. The doorman pushed the door open, not without effort. Beyond the opening was a helicopter winding up.

Liberty didn't hesitate. She bolted for the open door. Cal almost called out but thought better of it. He followed after being ushered with the sweeping hand of the doorman.

When he slid into one of two passenger seats of the small aircraft, the pilot got to work winding the bird up the rest of the way. Cal shut the door and strapped himself in.

There were no instructions from the pilot. No headphones passed back for a chat. The best Cal could do was sit back and watch things unfold.

IT WAS LATER that night when the private plane, his third of the day, touched down. The lone stewardess opened the side door and extended the folding stairs.

"Welcome to Turks and Caicos, Mr. Stokes. Have a pleasant stay."

Tropical air blew into the confined space. Liberty sniffed at it, apparently intrigued.

Why Turks and Caicos? He hadn't been down to the island in years. But it only served to confirm a suspicion he had that

Wilcox's journey would be some twisted journey down memory lane. The theory went along with the little they knew about chameleon up to that point: Matthew Wilcox liked to make things personal, uncomfortably so.

Another car waited, this one a twenty-year-old taxi with a driver leaning against the side, a long cigarillo smoldering lazily between his lips.

"You got bags?" the driver asked with typical island charm, cigarillo bobbing in annoyance.

"Just these."

"Okay."

The driver slipped in and sparked the engine. Cal and Liberty piled in the back.

"Ever been to the islands?" the driver asked, letting out a long stream of smoke that made its way to the back seat.

"It's been a while."

"Here for vacation?"

"Business."

THEY REACHED the two-story beach house in just under thirty minutes. Impressive by Caribbean standards, the home stood untouched by the salt air laziness that permeated the country. Devoid of rust and mold, the proud building extended its welcome with a rambling drive and sheltered portico.

The driver whistled as they rolled up. "Nice place. Yours?"

"A friend's," Cal answered. Uttering that word to describe Wilcox made him feel like he needed to spit.

The cab coughed to a space under the portico.

"Here you go. Want help with the bags?"

"I'm good, thanks."

Cal tried to slip a tip over the front seat but the driver waved it away.

"Your friend took care of it. Enjoy your stay."

"Thank you."

"No problem. Hey, you go and visit Rum Tiki. My cousin's bar. Is down at the end of the beach. Best rum drinks on the island."

With that, the taxi sped away, belching a long stream of exhaust.

Liberty stayed glued to Cal's side as they waited. When it was obvious no one was coming to greet them, Cal said, "What do you say, girl? Go inside?"

Liberty's ears perked up at the question.

The front door stood open and Cal couldn't help but think that they were walking into a trap. He stepped inside, Liberty still at his side, sniffing at the air.

Cal's skin prickled. No gun, no problem, right?

There came a banging of pans from somewhere in the back of the house. Liberty froze at the sound.

Cal reached a hand down and stroked her back.

"Yeah. I feel it too."

As if on cue, a young man entered the main living area.

"Welcome." Wilcox's voice, no doubt. The voice was pinned to the cork board of Cal's mind, never to be taken down.

He was not handsome, but far from unpleasant. His face bore the signs of hard youth – narrow, skeptical eyes and the protective shield of a smirk. He looked younger than Cal, which was odd, as the man carried himself like an old soul, with measured steps and an air of confidence that comes only from a lifetime of corrected mistakes.

"We came," said Cal. "Now what?"

"Come on, buddy. Relax. It's the islands."

"I'm not really in the mood. Tell me what you want and — "

Wilcox raised a hand, impatience in his eyes. "You're my guest. I treat that title with respect. Now, dinner will be ready in fifteen minutes. Feel free to go to your room, unpack, shower."

Cal studied the angles. Escape routes out the massive side window. Hasty weapon made of the block of carved driftwood on the coffee table or the tarnished candlestick on the dining room table.

"Upstairs," Wilcox continued. "First door on the right. Your room, I mean."

Cal turned toward the winding staircase that overlooked the main room.

"Oh, before you go," Wilcox said. "I got you a welcome present."

Cal looked back to his host just in time to see something black flying through the air. He snatched it without thinking. It was a watch. A very nice watch.

"What am I supposed to do with this?"

"I thought maybe you could encase it in a shadowbox with all your other treasured memories of me."

Cal squinted at the man.

"You're supposed to *wear it*, Cal."

"I don't wear watches," Cal said, tossing the thing back.

Wilcox caught the watch in his left hand on a downswing, tossed it over his back and caught it in his right. He then tossed it back. "Relax. It's not coated in poison."

It took him a moment to figure out how the clasp worked. It was some sort of clicking mechanism with a release on the side. It cinched down the side of Cal's left wrist perfectly. Cal admired the various dials and turning pieces.

"GPS locator? You're gonna use this thing to track me?"

Wilcox shrugged and moved closer, walking like a being aware of every detail of the world around him, like the room parted as he passed by.

"First, it's a real watch. Second, it's waterproof. Third..." He lifted his shirt and pointed to his belt buckle. "It's an insurance policy. Watch. It's on level one. Tell me when you feel something."

Wilcox tapped the front of his belt buckle and Cal's left arm seized, not uncomfortably, just so it was impossible to control it. He couldn't even clench his fist.

Wilcox tapped his belt buckle again and the seizing stopped.

"No pain, right?"

He was right. Cal's arm felt normal, if a bit fatigued. He clenched his fist a couple times to make sure.

"Why not a shock collar?"

"It's not really in right now, fashion-wise. And in case you were thinking of somehow stripping me of my belt, my watch and a couple other devices control yours as well." Wilcox was quick to show, tapping the face of his own watch two times.

Cal's arm seized again. This time he felt a hint of pain, like the burrowing of a parasite.

Wilcox let him go with another tap on the belt buckle.

"Just so we're clear, you try to run, I've got you. You try to attack me, you go down." He looked down at Liberty who let out a low growl at the man. "And if she makes a move on me, same thing. Understand?"

Cal didn't think the question rated an answer.

Wilcox smiled, turned on his heel and headed back towards the kitchen. "Dinner's in exactly thirteen minutes and forty-three seconds. Don't be late. You've got a watch now. Use it."

CHAPTER EIGHT

Freshly showered, Cal stepped into the kitchen more curious than cautious. He wasn't sure why, but he believed that if Wilcox wanted him dead, he'd already be lying in the morgue.

This trip wasn't just about Wilcox's whims, it was about getting to the bottom of the mystery that was Wilcox.

"Right on time. I like that. Must be the Marine in you," Wilcox said without looking up from the cutting board. "I hope you like salmon. I picked this recipe up from a fantastic private chef in Punta Mita. Beer's in the fridge. Or there's a bar in the corner if you want something stronger."

Cal opted for a beer. Corona would do.

Wilcox tossed a lime slice over his shoulder. Cal caught it just in time.

"You mind pouring me a couple inches of Appleton?" Wilcox asked, scooping a handful of what looked like chives into a small bowl.

Cal walked over to the bar. There was a small assortment of your basic liquor needs. Vodka of Russian descent. Whiskey with a Japanese label. And finally, the eponymous Appleton rum.

Play along, Cal told himself. If only there was rat poison on the bar.

Cal was well aware of his own impatience with situations beyond his control. This special brand of impatience manifested itself in anger and barely-concealed rage. It helped on an op sometimes, but he'd come to realize in his sessions with Higgins that unmeasured portions of this rage often made its way into everyday life.

"You gonna pour that?" Wilcox asked from the kitchen.

Cal hadn't realized that he'd frozen with the bottle in hand. He shook off his ghosts and poured two inches of the amber liquid into a crystal rocks glass.

"Appleton your favorite?" Cal asked, trying out a little dialogue. Sometimes it was better to worm your way in through conversation.

"I find it useful to live like the locals. Gets me into the role. Don't you agree?"

"Sure." Cal walked back across the room and handed the glass to Wilcox.

His host took it and raised it back.

"To our time together. May it be fruitful."

Cal clinked his beer bottle against the crystal and they both took appreciative sips of their respective drinks.

"Can't say that it's my favorite, but it does pack a punch," Wilcox said as he set the glass down and got back to chopping. "Food's almost ready. Meet me out on the back porch?"

Cal nodded. He needed a few lungsful of fresh air. Another second with Wilcox might've sent him diving for the knife in the man's hand. He didn't know how far he would've gotten. Wilcox seemed completely in his element, occasionally flipping the blade in his hand before placing it on the counter.

Salt air greeted Cal when he stepped outside. He took a

second to close his eyes and inhale. The beach. The place made him think of Diane.

He opened his eyes and took in the sight. Crystal blue water. He estimated that visibility in the water went thirty feet down. Good snorkeling. Diane would've loved that.

Get a hold of yourself.

It wasn't uncommon for Cal to have thoughts of his ex, but now the memories crashed in.

What the hell is wrong with me?

Cal took a long pull from his beer, wishing the memories away. He gazed out over the white sand, observing the passersby. Couples walking hand in hand. A jogger running barefoot. A dark-skinned peddler toting his wares home.

Other than the errant passers, the beach was deserted. Private. Beautiful. Not that Cal felt the beauty. All he could feel was cold detachment. And so he continued analyzing the angles, searching for weaknesses in Wilcox's defenses.

"Dinner is served," came Wilcox's voice from the open door.

The table was set for two. Wilcox set two platters down. Ceviche flecked with the green of minced jalapeño on one and thin slices of salmon drizzled with dark brown liquid on the other.

"Which seat is yours?" Cal asked. Any question helped. He wanted to know Wilcox's quirks.

"Doesn't matter. I'm not picky."

Cal took the seat facing the beach. Wilcox the other.

"The ceviche is a local recipe. Picked it up my first trip here. Hope you don't mind a little spice. The salmon has a bit of ponzu drizzled over top. Please, you're the guest," he said, handing Cal one of the platters.

Cal began serving himself when Wilcox snapped his fingers.

"Almost forgot."

He sprang from the chair, almost causing Cal to do the same.

He was back a few moments later with a plastic bowl. Bending at the waist, Wilcox held the bowl out to Liberty.

"I hope she likes filet mignon. It's all I had."

Liberty sniffed from afar, cautious, tail still ramrod straight.

"Go ahead, girl. It's okay," Cal said.

Liberty cocked her head to one side as she looked to Cal for confirmation.

"Eat your food," Cal said, waving her towards the bowl that was now lying on the ground.

Hesitantly at first, Liberty padded forward, hackles raised. She licked the bowl. Then, as if finding it safe for consumption, she wolfed it down.

"I can pick up some dog food at the store tomorrow," Wilcox said, taking the platter back from Cal and serving himself.

"You don't have someone to do your shopping?"

Wilcox fixed him with a curious stare. "I'm not sure what you were expecting here, Cal. A house full of slaves? I'm not a monster, you know."

The poor dead bastards lying six feet under might say otherwise.

Cal bit back any retort and served himself a healthy heaping of ceviche. The food did look and smell delicious.

"Where did you learn how to cook? Your mother?"

"I see what you're doing."

"What?"

"We're not going there."

"Going where?"

Wilcox set his fork down. "Let's set some ground rules. No questions about my past. It's not germane to what we're doing here."

"What are we doing here?"

"We're having a very nice dinner on a very nice beach. Try the salmon. It's fantastic, I promise."

Cal wasn't hungry but he put a slice of raw salmon into his

mouth anyway. It was prepared to perfection and melted in his mouth.

"Very good," Cal heard himself concede.

"Told you. Now, to business."

"To business," Cal repeated, scooping ceviche onto his fork. It too was delicious. He looked down at Liberty, who was already finished with her dinner and rested contentedly next to her bowl.

"I'll bet you've been wondering why I kidnapped you and locked you in that freezing cell."

Cal froze, staring at his plate, fighting back a bit of bile that stirred inside him. "I assumed you wanted to kill me," he said flatly. He looked up at his host. Wilcox's face showed his disappointment.

"Now why would I want to do that?"

"We uncovered your plot. We exposed you to the world."

"You just don't get it, do you? I wanted that to happen. Call it my coming-out party. I'm not too proud to say that I wanted the headlines."

Cal forced a laugh. "So it was for the headlines. Ego."

"Oh, I don't care about that."

"You sure don't act like it. All this," Cal motioned to the house, to the food, to the beach, "it feels like some spoiled rich kid showing off."

Wilcox fixed a stare at him. "You know, Cal, I expected more from you. Especially after what I gave you."

"What, an all-expenses-paid trip to the beach? Thanks, but I can pay for my own vacations."

Now there was anger in Wilcox's eyes.

Good. Feel something you son of a bitch.

"Not the beach, what I gave you on that mountain."

Cal sat still, gauging Wilcox's demeanor.

"You're kidding."

"Why do you think I'm kidding?"

"You shut me in an ice cube to die and you think I owe you something?"

Wilcox's palm slapped down on the table, causing Liberty's head to spring up. "You're goddamned right you do. I can't believe you haven't figured it out by now. Maybe I was wrong. Maybe it's best if I just kill you."

Cal wasn't afraid to die, especially not now, but he wasn't going to sit there and take it.

"Tell me how you helped me, Wilcox," he said with a mocking lilt in his voice.

Wilcox ran his tongue over his teeth then spoke, short and measured.

"I gave you perspective on that mountain, you bastard. I tore you down to nothing so you could come back changed, better, the best version of yourself."

The bile stirred again. "Oh really. The best version of myself. Do you know what I've been through? Do you know what that mountain did to me?"

"Yeah. It *made* you."

Cal snorted. "*Made* me? You know what? You can shove your inner transformation bullshit up your ass. I'm leaving. Shock me if you want. Shoot me in the back of the head. I don't care anymore."

Cal rose and started walking away, expecting the jolt or the blazing pain of a gunshot at any moment. It didn't come.

Wilcox called after him. "That mountain brought you to this moment, Cal. I knew you'd survive. We're the same, you and I."

Cal stopped and turned back. "There's nothing in you that lives in me."

"Is that so? How about your little fight with Dante West? How do you explain that? A temporary lapse in judgment?"

"What do you know about West?" Cal asked, his blood at a steady flow.

Dante West. There wasn't a day that passed that Cal didn't hear the echo of that haunted name still resounding in his head.

"I know he was the drug lord that killed your fiancée. I know you tracked the scumbag down. A covert operation, was it?" He studied Cal's features, then smiled. "No, there was nothing of a covert op about it. You'd gone rogue, Cal. A vigilante. It wasn't an operation, it was a hunting expedition. It was Cal Stokes picking up where the lazy law had failed. You killed him, and rightfully so."

"I guess it wouldn't do any good for me to ask how you do your homework."

"Nope."

"Then I'll ask the next question. What the hell does all this have to do with what I did to West?"

"Bookends, Cal," Wilcox said calmly. "That was the beginning of your old life. This is the beginning of something new. I want to show you the *truth*."

"The truth, huh? And just what is the *truth* in your humble estimation?"

Wilcox shrugged. "The usual. Life and death. Black and white. Kill or be killed."

"Stop with the games, Wilcox."

"Fine. Then I want to show you what you're capable of."

Cal didn't know why, but the blunt statement struck a harmonious chord deep inside.

Wilcox continued. "You've noticed the changes. Your mind is sharper. Your reflexes are better than they've ever been. Why do you think that is?"

"Hard work."

Wilcox nodded. "That's part of it. But I alluded to the crux of what's happened before. I brought you down to the level zero. I tore your world down to nothing, just like you Marines do at Parris Island. You had nothing. You believed in nothing. There was only survival. You had two ways to go, either give up and die, or stand up and fight. I won the bet. I watched you for days, you know. I saw you reading your father's file. I saw you licking those walls, sleeping in fits and starts. Shivering from the cold. But I saw something else. Your fire. It never left. Till the day your friends found you. It was always there."

Cal tried to digest the words. He thought back to those terrible days, weeks. Struggled with his weakness, hoping for a savior.

"Why?" was the only question that escaped his lips.

"I told you. To make you better."

Breathe.

"You think you made my life better? You think this," he gestured to his body, "this is the best I can be? You can have it. I'm not playing your games."

"They're not games, Cal. This is life. Give me the weekend to show you."

Liberty's head was back down, resting on one paw. The sound of the beach and the smell of the salt. He looked at the watch on his wrist and something inside him made him chuckle. He was a prisoner, for all intents and purposes. But as long as he was here, Wilcox was his prisoner as well. Matthew Wilcox couldn't go anywhere without Cal Stokes. That was the thought he had that amused him.

"Okay," he said. "Show me."

CHAPTER NINE

Hours later, when the sun had fallen past the horizon, a knock rattled Cal from his sleep. Liberty went to the door with a growl.

"Time to go," Wilcox said from the other side.

Cal wiped his face with the back of his hand and looked at his watch. 2:30am.

"I'll be out in a minute."

When he emerged from his room, Wilcox was waiting, wearing a pair of swim trunks and bright orange shirt to match.

"Going to a pool party?" Cal asked.

Wilcox handed him a plastic bag. There were board shorts and a bright t-shirt inside.

"What do you want me to do with these?"

"Put them on."

"Seriously?"

"Do I look like I'm kidding?"

"As a matter of fact, you do. You look like some high school punk getting ready to pull the greatest prank of all time. Give me a minute."

He closed the door and looked down at Liberty. She cocked her head at his questioning gaze.

"Tell me about it, girl."

TWO MINUTES LATER, Cal emerged wearing colors he felt more than a little uncomfortable in.

"You look good," Wilcox said.

"I look like a pack of Starbursts. And so do you."

Cal took a sniff. Wilcox stunk of cologne. It reminded Cal of late night fraternity parties and trips to Panama City Beach.

"Doing your best Jersey Shore?" Cal asked.

Wilcox shrugged. "Gotta play the part. Oh, and the dog can't come. Sorry. They won't let her in."

"Why don't you let me take care of that."

Wilcox's eyes went from playful to cold. "This is one of those times that you need to listen to me. Leave the dog here, unless you want to lose her."

Cal met Liberty's eyes. Her ears drooped. It was like she knew what was coming.

"Back to the room, pup. Come on."

She took some urging, and the whining started as soon as he shut the door.

"She'll be safer here," Wilcox said, already turned to head to the stairs.

"Where are we going?"

Wilcox looked over his shoulder with a grin. "It's a surprise."

THE BAR WAS NO MORE than a tattered shack that looked pieced together with driftwood and bits of ocean detritus. A blinking neon sign called the place DRIFTER'S HAVEN. The party was in full swing when the taxi deposited Cal and his host at the curb.

He could smell the testosterone wafting off the place.

And he was right, as soon as they stepped into the bar, twenty pairs of eyes shifted to meet them, all male. Every inch of Cal's body was primed for confrontation, but he kept his outward countenance calm.

Wilcox stumbled forward, and for a moment Cal thought he's tripped on something. That was, until the man spoke in slurred patches to the bartender.

"A line of shots for my friend and I," Wilcox said sloppily, slithering onto a bar stool and scattering a handful of bills on the bar top. Not an eye in the place missed the move.

The bartender, a weathered rat with leathery dark skin, appraised the newcomers and then glanced at the bills on his workspace.

"Whatchu want?"

"How 'bout battery acid? My buddy here's developed a taste for it." Wilcox wheezed with fake laughter. "Jus' kiddin'. Whatever you got. We're too drunk to taste it anyway."

"Rum then," the bartender said, grabbing a bottle from the teetering shelf behind him.

"Rum. It's always rum here," Wilcox said, his slur so pronounced that even Cal had a hard time understanding.

Six shots sat waiting in their own puddles.

Wilcox lifted the first and turned to the rest of the room. "To all of you fine folks."

Cal saw one head shake, another turn to a friend and whisper something. This was a working-class joint, with men just in from sea, or fresh off jobs laboring in some shithole somewhere nearby. They were dirty and lean, all working muscle. He and Wilcox, dressed like privileged partying trash, were as out of place here as two people could be.

"Come on, buddy," Wilcox said, handing a shot to Cal. "Don't you love this place. Quaint right? Like a slaughterhouse in August."

The bartender scowled at Wilcox.

Cal took the shot and downed it without blinking. He set it down on the bar and grabbed another. Might as well go along with the play.

"A line of shots for our fellow bar mates right here to my left," Cal said, pushing a couple bills towards the bartender. That piqued the interest of two men sitting closest to the companions. "Whadya say, pardner?"

The man next to Wilcox nodded, the edge in his animosity-laced eyes waning. Free booze does that to man.

"As a matter of fact," said Wilcox, "give one to everybody. I don't discriminate, no matter how stinky you may be."

The offering, despite its side of condescension, calmed the room. Conversation resumed and the bartender went to his duties around the room, pouring but rarely clearing.

Twenty minutes and three rounds later, two more customers sauntered into the bar. They seemed more weathered than the old bartender, if that was possible. But what really caught Cal's eye were the long knives hanging from each of their waistbands.

Wilcox didn't even seem to register their presence, although the newcomers were quick to size up to the two Americans. Cal ignored them too.

Their staring complete, the newbies found a seat at the back of the room, conveniently given up by an extremely large man who skittered away at the simple nod of one of the knife carriers.

The bartender turned all smiles, the perfection of proprietorship, for the two men. They ordered beers, libations Cal was sure the two men would not be paying for.

Cal watched the bartender work, carefully selecting beers

from the very bottom of the cooler, the coldest of the selection. The very best for his newest clientele.

Four bottles balanced on the tray, the bartender careful as he slipped by the teetering Wilcox. To Cal's surprise, Wilcox swiveled around in the blink of an eye and grabbed one of the bottles. It was a testament to the bartender's skills that he recovered so quickly. Not one of the three remaining bottles fell to the sandy floor.

Before the man could protest, Wilcox jumped to his feet. "You!" he pointed straight at the larger of the newcomers, the man's bulging eye twitching. He never had a chance. With one fluid movement, Wilcox flipped the bottle in his hand, gripped the neck, and threw it at the man.

Time slowed. Wilcox grinned. The bottle smashed into the man's forehead, not with the crash of Hollywood sugar glass, but with the thunk of thick glass on solid oak.

The crash came when Wilcox's target fell to the floor.

Now eyes turned from left to right. Shock. Excitement. A crowd ready for a brawl.

The downed man's companion looked larger when he rose from his chair. The knife came out without hesitation.

The next piece of surprise came when Wilcox fell to the floor, seemingly unconscious. But when Cal bent down to see if he'd been hit by a silent bullet or flying beer bottle, Wilcox winked at him.

No time to think. The behemoth's stomping charge was coming.

Cal twisted from his squatting position just in time to see the blade arching down. So much for a friendly night out on the town.

On a normal day, Cal wouldn't have a hard time taking the man down. Sure, he was taken unaware to a point. Sure, he was squatting. Sure, he didn't have a single weapon on his person.

But something turned in him. Some feeling he'd only felt in fits and starts in the past. Something primal, no thought needed.

Cal slid to the side and the blade came down. It thunked into the bar stool he'd just been sitting on, cleaving straight through.

No time to think on that. Cal went with the fluidity, the flow of his thoughts and the movement of his body as one. His right elbow caught the attacker in the back of the knee, toppling the man in one strike. Cal watched in morbid fascination as the man planted, face first, into the edge of the bar.

Game over.

He checked to make sure the man wasn't dead. Nope. Still breathing, although he'd have a helluva headache when he woke.

Cal turned back to the room and found it stirring, the wolves smelling the kill.

"Stay back," Cal warned, rising to his feet.

Another couple of tentative steps forward came the crowd.

Cal counted twelve.

For some reason the number didn't matter.

He scanned each and every one in the blink of an eye. No weapons that he could detect.

How had he done that? So fast. So complete was his analysis that he could only wonder.

A thought for another day.

Two came as one, in a rush thinking to take Cal in their wake.

Forearms raised for the bulrush, they rushed in.

So slow, Cal thought. *Like the Matrix.*

He pulled the same move. Instead of going left or right, he went down. Who would do that?

He would.

Total surprise... and pain.

These men weren't his enemies, but they were. They all were.

He attacked with cold calculation, losing himself to the savagery.

Cal's leg swept one to the ground, and at the next split-second his fist smashed into the next man's groin.

One. Two. Down.

All you could hear were the groans, though Bob Marley was singing a rousing rendition of *No Woman No Cry* on the jukebox in the corner.

Cal stood again.

"Anyone else?"

No one spoke.

Sirens in the distance. Cal glanced at the bartender who shrugged as if to say, "Why would I call the cops?"

"Sorry for the mess," Cal said.

Wilcox was up and moving again. He searched the guy who'd split the barstool with his machete. Cal saw him take something from the man's front pocket and put it in his own. Then, with that same grin of glee, Wilcox looked at Cal and said, "We're good to go."

CHAPTER TEN

Please, God, help Father Francis.

The good priest was being held by the neck, his face turning an uncomfortable shade of red.

Pindip watched from his hiding spot, a recessed nook on the second story of the church. He'd used it often, people-watching for hours at a time. It was a perfect hiding spot. No one bigger could even fit through the hole in the roof.

"Where is he?" the overgrown ape demanded of the priest. Pindip saw spittle hit the priest's face and thought that maybe the big man was on drugs.

"I don't know," the priest managed to squeak out.

He was surrounded by a gang of five. Local hoods with deeper ties, Pindip knew. Behind them was the plumber, the same one who'd come to fix the toilets. This one watched and nibbled at his fingertips as the priest was bullied and questioned.

Please, Father, bring my angel to help.

His angel. The man who had saved him and brought him to safety. His angel, the man who came at odd times, to pitch in at the church and slip the priest money by the handful.

Father Francis said that God answered prayers, but the angel didn't come.

"He hasn't been here in weeks," said Father Francis. The brave priest was close to breaking.

"That's a lie," the plumber shouted. A crowd of curious onlookers gathered now, poor townsfolk whose only source of entertainment for the day would be the humiliation of a humble holy man. "He was just here."

"No," the priest pleaded. "I never know when he's coming."

"He's lying," the plumber said. "He knows how to contact him."

Now the ape lifted the priest off the ground. "Tell me, priest. Where is the American?"

He was pressing too hard. *Too much*, Pindip thought.

Something in the boy snapped, and Pindip rushed from his hiding spot, down the stairs and toward the front door of the church. His fellow orphans cowered there, a dozen of them ranging from five years in age to fifteen. Some stared from the window. Others hid behind pews.

"Come with me!" Pindip yelled as he ran to the front door. No one moved. He whirled around. "We must help him." Still no one moved. Pindip locked eyes with one particularly rambunctious teen who'd been forgiven too many times to count by the priest. He liked to act tough, use his size to bully the younger kids. Now Pindip saw only fear.

"Cowards," Pindip whispered. He felt like spitting at them.

Back to the door he ran, casting it open, the sunlight hitting his face, and he sprinted into the daylight.

All faces turned at the sound. Pindip, rage in his veins, ran toward the gathering. The ape eyed him with mild amusement. The priest's eyes met Pindip's. Pindip thought he saw a smile there. The ape must have noticed too, because he lowered his captive to the ground.

"Look," said the plumber, a cruel laugh in his voice, "one of the bastards is here to claim the body."

The priest was on the ground, his usually pristine vestments now soaking up mud from last night's rain.

"Father," Pindip said, cradling the priest's head in his lap.

Nothing.

"Father!"

He shook the man's head. No response. His tiny hand reached out and tried to press on the older man's chest. That's what they did in the movies. There was a snicker from above. The plumber.

"That's what he deserves," the plumber said, spitting on the priest's leg.

Pindip laid the priest's head gently on the ground, repositioning himself so he could press the man's chest. They did that too. They put their hands on the chest and they pressed over and over. And soon the body jerked up with a breath and a cough and threw its arms around you, and then got up and joined in with the fight. It happened all the time.

His little hands pumped. There were murmurs in the crowd.

"Here, now, leave him," said a voice.

Pindip kept pressing, pumping, splattering the face with his tears.

"I said leave him," the plumber said more forcefully, reaching down and yanking the boy off the body. "He's dead, for Christ's sake."

Something bright and red flashed inside the boy's head, in his mind. It came up from his heart, and it burned – hot. Then the flash made his body numb and moved his feet and his arms. It made terrible sounds come from his throat. And it made him smash at the plumber with his fists. Over and over again.

"He's going to kill you!" cried Pindip. "He'll kill you!"

The plumber laughed, trying frantically to get hold of the

boy's flailing arms, and occasionally let out a string of curses when an errant fist hit home.

"That's enough," the plumber screamed.

Pindip backed off, his breath coming in tearing rasps. His rage spoke for him. "He'll kill you!"

"What are you talking about, you little bastard?" He pointed at the lifeless figure on the ground. "He's already dead."

"Not him," Pindip said in a hiss. "My angel. He will find you, and he will kill you."

CHAPTER ELEVEN

"You wanna tell me what the hell that was about?" Cal asked.

They'd left the bar without a word. No one else had taken up the mantle of hero for their fallen comrades.

"All in due time, my friend."

"This your thing?"

"What do you mean?" said Wilcox, walking one pace ahead like he had somewhere important to be. The rest of his body language gave nothing away, just another tourist in paradise.

Cal hopped once to lock in step. "You like picking fights with locals. You get off on it."

Wilcox shook his head.

"No?" said Cal.

"No."

"Then what is it?"

"Patience, Cal."

It was pitch black and Wilcox looked just as home in the dark as he did in the sunlight. For some reason that made Cal think of Daniel.

No. They weren't the same.

Cal estimated it had taken close to thirty minutes to get to their destination. The small port looked like it had been carved out of the Turks coast with a shovel. Sheer walls of dirt cut straight down to the water.

One rickety pier held a single fishing vessel swaying in the evening tide.

"This is us," Wilcox said, making no effort to stay concealed.

"What is it?"

Wilcox put a finger to his lips. "Shh."

There were more than a few slats missing on the dock. They had to hop lightly.

The boat was about forty feet in length, enough to carry a crew of ten on a fishing charter. A hundred years of warm fish and puke greeted their nostrils as they approached.

Wilcox reached out to touch the hull. He stood frozen. Listening? Cal heard nothing except the gentle lapping of sea water.

"Come on."

Wilcox hopped onboard, more careful now. Cal followed. He felt naked and exposed.

They maneuvered from the side to the small bridge. Wilcox flicked on a couple of lights that lit up the boat like a beacon.

Cal gritted his teeth. So much for secrecy.

Down to the cabin. The steps were slick, untended. The owners, presumably the guys from the bar, were poor owners.

Wilcox took something out of his pocket and held it up for Cal to see. A key.

"Magic time," Wilcox said, reaching out and putting the key in the cabin's lock.

A smell flooded out as soon as the door opened. Sweat. And fear.

The hairs on the back of Cal's neck stood on end. The sixth

sense that had kept him alive on so many missions was urging him to reach out and pull Wilcox back.

In went the assassin, quiet as the night.

Cal waited.

He heard whispering.

Then a sniffle.

Cal stepped inside. It took a few moments for his eyes to adjust in the gloom. He could just make out Wilcox's shape at the far side of the space. The place was as much a mess as the upper deck. Life preservers scattered and piled. Old fishing gear stacked in haphazard spots throughout the room. It was more spacious than Cal had expected. It must've run the length of the boat. Perfect for hauling.

Cal moved closer to where Wilcox looked like he faced a wall. Who was he whispering to?

"It's okay," Wilcox said. Not to him. To someone else here. When Cal finally saw who that someone else was, his blood went thick.

Ten, maybe fifteen children were packed into a cage. Some whimpering. Others crouched and staring with dead eyes.

"It's okay," Cal heard himself saying. The children came in all sizes and shapes, although most were dark in complexion. From the islands or somewhere else?

Wilcox got the cage door open and edged it over with a creak.

"Come on. We won't hurt you," he said, beckoning the children out.

"What the hell..." Cal started to ask. Wilcox had put a finger to his lips.

"Come on," Wilcox said, gently urging the children out. "Are you hungry?" He made the universal sign for eating. That got them moving.

The stench of their grubbiness was almost too much to bear. Cal resisted the urge to hold his breath or cover his nose with his shirt. He'd seen all manner of evil, but the pathetic sight cut to his core. It was impossible now to focus on his enemy.

With some coaxing, they got the children to follow them upstairs. Wilcox directed Cal to scrounge a meager stack of cookies and sodas from a cooler on deck. Not one of the children rushed for the food. They waited patiently, though expectantly.

When was the last time they'd eaten?

When they were given food, they ate with nervous glances between bites. Stray animals hunched over their good fortune.

"Who are they?"

"Cubans."

Cal shook his head. "Where are their parents?"

Wilcox widened his eyes. "Not in front of the kids," he said. His eyes cast a sideways glance at the children. "At any rate, you know what happened to the parents."

Once the meager meal was complete, Wilcox went to the console and started the engine. Every child shrank to the deck, shaking.

"It's okay," said Wilcox. "*Estas seguro.*" You're safe.

It wasn't a long ride. Fifteen minutes later, the boat approached a much more impressive pier. A huge yacht stood waiting.

There was a scurry of activity as the smaller boat approached. Not the starched perfection of yacht deck hands, but a middle-aged band of helpers who helped Wilcox tie his newly acquired skiff to the pier.

"How many are there?" a woman with sun-streaked hair asked, all business.

"Sixteen," Wilcox said, handing the smallest passenger over to her.

"Any problems?"

"None."

No more talking. The children were transferred from the boat to the pier to the yacht. The only words Cal heard were the murmurings of soothing from adults to children. The kids were tentative at first, gazing up at the yacht like they'd just arrived at Disney World.

Cal pointed to the people on the yacht. "Who are *they?*"

"Them? Those are the good guys. Come on. We've got another stop to make." Wilcox jumped from the boat to the wood ramp.

The woman with sun-streaked hair appeared again carrying a small manila envelope.

"Ah," said Wilcox, receiving the envelope as if he'd almost forgotten it. "Thanking you kindly. I'll be in touch."

No word from the woman, who turned away as if ordered.

Cal's stomach twisted looking at Wilcox holding the envelope, and reality hit him. In the dramatic sway of the evening's events, he'd somehow deluded himself into believing that Wilcox had saved the children for the right reason. As crazy as it sounded in his head, Cal had actually believed Wilcox was capable of the altruistic act.

"Who smacked you with a wet fish?" Wilcox said.

"Let's go," Cal said, turning to leave.

"You don't even know where we're going."

"The boat's hot, so I assume we're not taking that. My guess is we're walking."

Wilcox flipped the envelope to Cal.

It wasn't heavy, barely more than the weight of the envelope itself.

"Open it."

He opened the clasp and dumped the contents into his hand. A key chain with a single key attached.

"You thought it was money, didn't you?"

Cal said nothing and looked backed down at his hand.

"You still think I'm a monster."

Wilcox waited a beat, and then exhaled.

"Come on. You're driving."

He headed back onto land without further explanation. And Cal Stokes followed, determined to get into the mind of Matthew Wilcox..

CHAPTER TWELVE

The car was a foreign model Cal didn't recognize. One of those ubiquitous refrigerator boxes that rolled over the islands of the Caribbean. Pure functionality without the luxuries of the western world. Not even a radio.

"Take a left up ahead," Wilcox ordered.

It was the fifth turn they'd taken. Cal was usually adept at staying aware of his surroundings, but whether it was darkness, the fact that Wilcox had them touring in circles, or just that the basic road system was a far cry from that of a major U.S. city, Cal had no idea where the hell they were going.

A squat series of buildings appeared up ahead. A small strip mall that'd seen better days. A single street lamp illuminated the pockmarked parking lot.

"Pull in there."

Cal did as instructed, slowing to receive Wilcox's next command. None came, so Cal parked in the farthest space, away from the buildings.

"This is fine. Turn off the car but leave the key in the ignition," Wilcox said, following the assertion by slipping out of the car. "Come on, son. Chop chop."

"Chop chop, your ass," Cal mumbled.

IT WAS A SLOW, careful trudge through flora and fauna after that. Wilcox moved like a creature of the night, mindful of every branch, stepping lightly and with only the slightest hint of noise. Cal felt like an overburdened mule in comparison. Again, Cal thought of Daniel. He and Wilcox could've been twins in the sneaking department.

He could feel the approach of daylight as they pushed deeper into the vegetation. Then came the sound of lapping waves. They were on the coast again. Another boat?

His question was answered moments later when a two-story structure came into view. The place was lit up like a roman candle and the thumping of bass hit their ears as they approached. It was muted, as if the windows were a foot thick.

"This is the tricky part," Wilcox said, hopping a short stone fence. There was another taller, concertina wire-lined barrier up ahead.

The large home wasn't a fortress, but Cal was sure that there were safety measures scattered through the property.

Wilcox trudged on with unbridled determination. When he reached the base of the tall wall, he bent down and fiddled with something on the ground.

"Grab the other side," he said, handing the end of what looked like a tarp to Cal.

It was heavy, like an oversized sleeping mat.

Wilcox motioned with his head to the top of the wall. "Up and over."

Now Cal got it. The way through the concertina. Wilcox starting swinging the mat forward then back, getting a rhythm.

"One, two, *three*."

On three they swung the mat hard, up and onto to the wall, covering a portion of the concertina. Their way in.

"You first," Wilcox said breathily, making a step with his interlocked hands.

Cal had visions of rabid dogs waiting on the other side. He stepped into Wilcox's hands and heaved up. Sliding up and over, Cal perched on his belly, turning, careful to avoid the razor wire. He reached back the way he'd come, grasping Wilcox's hand when he jumped. It was like they'd done it a thousand times.

In short order they were on the other side. Their new position gave Cal a direct view of the opulence of the place. The grounds were immaculate, more Japanese garden than island getaway; a brand-new four-wheeler parked in the corner, resplendent with shiny chrome wheels; a stack of pool inflatables and a pair of jet skis.

They slid around the side of the house, more toys along the way. Everything was parked in its place, neat and tidy. Like a very organized child lived in the getaway.

"Put on a smile," Wilcox whispered.

"What?"

"Put on a smile. You look too serious."

"You're kidding, right?"

"You're no fun, you know that? Honestly, I don't know how they deal with you."

They'd made it to the square-cut pool in the front yard that overlooked the beach. It glowed blue with underwater lighting. An inflatable white swan drifted aimlessly across the pool.

"Let's go in and join the party, shall we?"

Cal expected cameras, security, at least a locked door. They found none of the above. They stepped right inside.

Marble floors and purple flowers on the table next to a set of car keys. The place was open, luxurious, but tastefully appointed in the modern trends. Clean lines. Edges of silver and gold. Nothing too over the top. Just fancy enough.

A guy sauntered into the room carrying a bowl, a scoop of what looked like cereal making its way into his mouth. The man, who looked more like a kid just hitting adolescence, froze, eyes wide. At least he had the wherewithal to finish his bite and not drop the bowl.

Eyes wary, but not scared. "Who are you?" he asked, somewhat composed.

"We're here to save your life," Wilcox answered like a used car salesman.

"What?"

"I said we're here to save your life. In exactly five minutes, a trio of Russian assholes is gonna bust through that door. When I say bust, I'm exaggerating. The door's already unlocked. That's how *we* got in."

"But my — "

"Security system? I'd get my money back on that one if I were you."

The guy shuffled, looking around.

"Okay. What do you want?"

"We'll talk about that later. Let's get you to your safe room. My buddy and I will take care of the Russians."

Wilcox had known not only the location of the safe room, but the combination as well. That had really set the kid back on his heels. Now safely ensconced, brand new code entered just in case, the two companions were standing in the kitchen, looking at the impressive array of weapons in the secret compartment at the very back of the pantry.

"I'd prefer something, lighter, but I'll take this one," Wilcox said, grabbing an AR-15 modified with a variety of upgrades hitched to its composite length. "What about you?"

"This is a joke, right?"

"Why, is something funny?"

Cal shook his head. It all felt like a bad dream. "That kid, this place, it's..."

"Unbelievable?"

"That was the exact word I was going to use."

"Look, Cal, let's take care of this guy's problem and then we'll discuss it, okay?"

Wilcox glanced at his watch. "Thirty seconds. You better hurry up and choose."

Cal exhaled, still not sure if someone was going to jump from a hidden room and yell, Surprise!

He chose a compact submachine gun. It felt good in his hands. Decent caliber. He checked the chamber and the magazine. Loaded and ready.

"Okay. Now what?"

Wilcox put up a finger and closed his eyes. He was tapping his foot on the ground, like counting bars.

"And... now."

The explosion of glass from the main room stunned Cal for a split second.

Wilcox put on his best joker's smile. "Come on. Let's have some fun."

CHAPTER THIRTEEN

The forms streamed in one at a time.

One. Two. Three.

A pause and two more slipped in.

All men. None masked. All with the look of hardened war veterans and criminals, tattoos plastered down their arms.

One of them said something in Russian and sprayed the living room with his weapon. No targets there.

More Russian from the leader. They split in two groups, the group of three coming straight for the kitchen.

Wilcox was still grinning. He even winked at Cal before skidding to the side of the counter. His rounds took the first man in the legs, the Russian idiot depressed his own trigger to send flurry of bullets into the ceiling. The wounded man screamed and fell to the ground.

No time like the present, Cal thought.

He went out the other side, finding his target in no time.

Two shots in the man's chest. The Russian stopped in his tracks, not even looking down at his chest, but looking right at Cal. His weapon was already up.

Cal didn't hesitate. Two more shots took the man square in

the face. Easy day. No staring back now. The man's eyes were gone in a bloody mess as he collapsed to the floor.

"You get the third. I'll go for the other two," Wilcox yelled. There was no hurry in his voice, just detached amusement.

The third man was closer to Cal anyway, swiveling toward the Marine. Cal saw Wilcox run from the kitchen. It was impossible to miss him in his bright clothes, the college partier gone to save the day.

Number three growled something in Russian as Cal put just enough pressure on the perfectly calibrated trigger. Sweet. Maybe he'd take this baby home with him.

Another burst from his weapon, the kill shot.

Three down.

Shooting from another room. Screams of pain and curses in Russian.

Cal was up and moving, scanning for new additions as he went. Wilcox had said three intruders but there'd been five. Was that an outright lie or was his intel screwy?

No time for those kinds of questions. *Focus.*

Deeper into the house he went. More screams.

He followed the bullet trail along the walls. It looked like someone wanted to send a message to anyone who found the place: Not only will we shoot you, but we'll shoot every wall and trinket that you have.

He passed the body of a fourth Russian, bleeding from a dozen wounds onto the once-shiny marble floor. Cal approached the bedroom with the safe room tucked inside a massive walk-in closet.

Two more shots.

Faster now. Get there to see the ending. All he had to do now was follow the blood trail.

Another scream, this the deepest yet.

He got to the room, glanced inside. Wilcox had the last intruder standing against the wall, arms in the air.

"There you are," Wilcox said without looking away from his catch. "Any problems in the kitchen?"

"No," Cal said.

"Good. Lookee what we've got here. Igor was about to talk, weren't you, Igor."

The Russian sneered. His left arm hung limp at his side, blood dripping down onto the plush carpet.

"I asked you a question, Igor. You don't want another shot in the arm, do you?"

A brief look of panic in the big man, which he then hid as fast as it had come, puffing his chest out.

"Kill me, American pig," he said.

Wilcox let out a string of Russian.

The wounded man's face went pale.

Wilcox smiled. "There. Now we're on the same page. Cal, I just told our friend Igor that his only surviving relative, an uncle who used to be a KGB goon, *now* spends his time drooling on himself, and is, as we speak, being strapped down to have his limbs sawed off his body."

Cal looked from Wilcox to the Russian. One man was clearly enjoying the standoff more than the other.

"You lie," the Russian said, this time with much less bravado.

"You think so?" Wilcox rattled off an address. Again, the Russian's face paled.

"How you know this?"

Wilcox let out of hearty laugh. "You have no idea who you chose to fuck with, comrade."

The Russian looked toward the safe room.

"No, not him, you idiot. Us."

"Who are you?" Igor asked.

"I'm Crockett, he's Tubbs. And you've come to witness the

beginning of a very profitable relationship. Now, tell me, where are the rest of your men? In the black van parked on the street?"

Igor nodded.

"And will they come help you if they heard the shooting?"

Igor hesitated. Wilcox did not. A single trigger pull spat a round that hit the Russian in the left thigh, sending the man to one knee. Tough bastard.

"No, no. They stay in van."

"See? Telling the truth isn't that hard, is it?" He leaned down. "Is it, Igor?"

Igor shook his head, gritting his teeth through the pain.

"Last question." This time Wilcox asked it in Russian. Whatever he said made Igor look up. His face changed, more confident now.

"You crazy, American."

"That's what some say. Answer the question, Igor. Uncle Vlady is waiting."

Igor answered the question in Russian, short clipped words.

"Good. Thank you very much for your cooperation, my friend." Wilcox took two steps forward. He was within arm's reach of the Russian, a fact not lost by the kneeling man. He took his opportunity, lunging at Wilcox.

Cal saw Wilcox's face. He actually shook his head, his face twisted in disappointment, like a parent upset that junior still isn't in bed.

A spanking was coming.

It came in the form of a simple step to the side and a casual two rounds from Wilcox's weapon that took Igor in the side of the head.

Game over, Igor.

"Well, that was fun. Let's go talk to our buddy in the closet."

Cal stayed near the door, still wary of the men Wilcox had

mentioned in the van. They could rush the house at any time, despite what Igor had said.

Combination punched in, the reinforced door eased open. The pale face of the house's owner appeared.

"Come on out," Wilcox said, waving to the room.

"I heard gunshots," the kid said. Then he saw the body, doubled over and puked on the floor.

"Well, I wasn't expecting that," Wilcox said. "Come on. Stand up and look at the mess you've made." He reached down and helped him stand at full height. "You know who they are, right?"

The kid's lip trembled and he was just able to get out, "Russians," before bending over and expelling the rest of his dinner.

"Righto. Now, we don't have much time. There are at least two more KGB wannabes in a van on the street. It's time to talk fee."

"What?"

"Fee. You know, as in money, payment for services rendered."

"You want me to pay you? For what?"

Wilcox waved at the body on the ground.

"For saving your ass."

"But..."

"No buts, no nuts, no coconuts, pal. I've seen your account. Enough crypto currency to keep you rolling in Funyons for the rest of your life."

The kid shook his head, maybe clearing the nausea, maybe clearing his thoughts. "Who the hell are you guys?"

"I'm Smith, he's Wesson. But what really matters now is that we get this transaction completed before you join your would-be kidnapper in hell."

It didn't take long. Another glance at the bleeding body of Igor and the kid capitulated.

Cal wasn't up on his cyber currency, but from the look on the kid's face, whatever he'd just agreed to pay Wilcox was a majority of his wealth. Finally, the deal was concluded.

"See, that wasn't so hard. And don't worry kid, I have faith in your skills. You'll make your money back. You wily computer geeks always do. Impressive really. Wish I'd paid more attention in school."

"Seriously, man, who are you?"

Wilcox's face went serious. He got almost nose to nose with the cowering kid.

"I'm someone you never want on your front porch again. So, if you want to avoid Igor's fate, stick to legal pursuits. That means no more hookers, no more deals with the Russians, the Chinese, or the Saudis. You got that?"

"But, how could you...?"

The weapon came up, muzzle pressed to the kid's forehead.

"You're not as smart as I thought you'd be in person."

"Yeah, yeah. I get it. Stay inside the lines. No out of the box deals."

Wilcox grinned, planted a kiss on the kid's forehead where his muzzle had just been.

"See? Who says kids can't learn from their elders?" Wilcox looked at his watch. "Well, we better get going. Nobody else is gonna take care of those assholes in the van. Better get back to work."

"What am I supposed to do about the dead bodies?" the kid asked in renewed desperation.

"You're a smart cookie. Figure it out."

Wilcox joined Cal at the door, then turned to the cowering kid. "Oh, and one more thing. If you even think about mentioning us to the cops, the Feds, anyone... well, you know what happens."

Igor was all the evidence the kid needed.

· · ·

THERE WAS no one in the waiting van. No reinforcements.

"What about the other guys?" Cal asked as Wilcox got in the driver's seat.

"What other guys?"

"The guys you said were in this van. The reinforcements."

Wilcox grinned. "You think they needed reinforcements to take down that pansy?"

Cal shook his head and got in the passenger side. The back of the van was completely empty. No gear. No trash. Nothing.

They took off down the road and drove for a few minutes in silence. A ramshackle gas station awaited them as the sun crested the horizon, sweet sunlight coming to Turks and Caicos for yet another day.

"What's this? Another take down?" Cal asked.

"Nope. Gotta get rid of the van."

An ancient man with the skin the color of petrified chocolate baked by a century in the sun met them at the pump.

"Hey, Pops!" Wilcox said, jumping from the van and tossing the keys to the old man. To Cal's surprise, the shuffling old-timer snatched the keys out of the air without a twitch.

"It got gas?"

"About half a tank."

"Anything in the back?"

"Nope. She's all clean and she's all yours."

Pops nodded, taking a quick tour around the van to do his own inspection. He pulled a screw driver from his pocket and went to work on the license plate.

"Same deal as before, Pops," Wilcox said.

The old man looked up through rheumy eyes. "You don't want nothin' for it?"

"Nah. Just got my paycheck. I'll be in touch, okay?"

"Sure. Sure."

"You tell the sister I said hello."

"Yah, mon."

Wilcox waved and they were off, walking down the dirt trail that led back to the main drag.

"It's a couple miles back home. You up for the hike, Marine?"

"Yeah," Cal said without looking at his companion.

"Hey, come on, don't be so down in the mouth. We did good tonight. You did good."

A few more steps and Cal asked, "What *did* we do tonight?"

"Like I told Pops, we got paid."

"So, blackmail."

"Call it what you want, Cal. I call it saving the day. Do you have any idea what those Russian goons would've done to that kid? Those guys were professional stickup artists. Only not in your traditional sense. They find these rich cyber kids and torture them until they transfer all their money to their accounts. Sometimes they let them go. Sometimes they don't."

"Why?"

"Because they're sick bastards, that's why."

"No, why are you doing this?"

Wilcox looked up at the brightening sun, closed his eyes for a second and smiled. "Life is short, Cal Stokes. Might as well get to livin' it."

Wilcox did not explain further, once again leaving Cal to ponder his captor's motives.

CHAPTER FOURTEEN

CAL'S JOURNAL

I've never written in a journal before. Doc Higgins suggested I do it and Briggs seconded the notion, after the fact, of course.

Wilcox, while being some kind of crazy lunatic, at least gives me the run of his house. I found this paper in his office when he was gone. See I'm rambling now. No idea what to write.

Wilcox could find this tonight, tomorrow, and then what? The guy has all my deepest darkest thoughts?

Don't know why I'm doing this. Maybe it's because I can't talk to Liberty about it.

I'll admit, I need a release, need to get some things out. Maybe I'll crumple this paper up and burn it before Wilcox comes home.

Yeah, you heard that right, Dear Diary, that was me sighing. Feel like I've been doing a lot of that.

Now don't misunderstand me, I'm not feeling sorry for myself. Honestly, if you think that stint in the mountain broke me, you're wrong. Sure I wasn't myself for a while, but Higgins assured me it's perfectly normal.

I've been through what shrinks call traumatic experiences before. I've been shot. Those closest to me have been killed. The worst of the worst in many people's lives. Truly crappy.

But this time is different. There's something in me that feels... not broken. It's hard to explain. Like I said, not broken... new.

I know Wilcox sees it. He alluded to it just like my closest friends see it.

My reflexes are better than they've ever been. A lot of guys get tunnel vision in tactical situations. I never have, but now... In that house with the cyber kid, I saw everything. I swear I could've heard a cockroach scurrying up the stairs.

Okay, that's an exaggeration. Imagine you've lived your entire life only seeing half of a picture. It's a pretty picture, maybe with a cozy little house with a quaint picket fence. It's there. It's real.

Then one day you find out that there's another half of the picture, something that's been hidden the entire time. Not only is there one house, there's two. Not identical. Completely unique. No picket fence but a swing wrapped around the thick branches of the oak out front.

You knew the story of the family that lived in the first house. You know their names, how old they are, what they like on their pancakes.

Now, after realizing there's another house next door, you want to know about the family living just feet from the first family. Who are they? What do they like on their pancakes? How are they connected to the first family?

So many questions.

I'm not sure if that explains it in the right words. It's not like I'm a writer. Just a dumb grunt trying to figure out what the hell is going on.

So yeah, I'm looking at the world through different lenses now. No more standard definition. I'm all HD. Every tiny blemish, every color combination. I see it. I feel it.

I should've asked Daniel about it but there wasn't time. There never seems to be enough of that, you know? Where does it go? We get older and bit by bit it slips by until finally life feels like a tidal wave swooshing by.

There you go. I've gone and done it. Top would laugh. He'd say I'm turning into a poet.

Ha.

I don't know what I'm turning into, and maybe that scares me.

No, scare is the wrong word.

You hear that? That's me tapping this pencil on the desk trying to figure out how I feel.

Tap, tap, tap.

I'm getting closer to understanding, I think. Maybe it's that nothing scares me anymore. I've taken the deep dive and come up for air. I know the mysteries of the cave, or at least I think I do.

But where does that leave me?

I'll tell you where it leaves me, with Wilcox in this damn house.

The guy acts more like my best friend than the guy who black-mailed my friends and me. He keeps looking at me with some sort of an expectation, like he's waiting for me to say something. What? Thanks? Go to hell?

But I'm not angry. Is that weird? Shouldn't I be mad at the guy who used my face to kill? You have no idea what a problem that caused for me. I won't give you the details here. Pointless anyway.

So yeah, I'm not mad.

Tap, tap, tap.

And now here I sit, realizing with blazing clarity that I'm actually enjoying this.

CHAPTER FIFTEEN

Visitors came and went. The odd delivery arrived and the proprietor of the meager establishment came to the door, half the time cursing, receiving packages large and small.

Pindip watched it all from one of a dozen places. He was good at hiding. He'd learned it from his years as a street rat. The lessons hadn't been hard to slip back into – like an old shirt you thought you'd never wear again since it was worn and patched in places, yet dependable and ready for hard work.

The plumber. He'd started it all. He was Pindip's target. There was nothing the little boy could do, of course. He was no murderer. It wasn't what Father Francis would've wanted. Father Francis. Dead now. Thrown in a heap of trash. The villagers were told. No, not told, *ordered* not to bury the priest like he deserved.

Desecration.

Pindip remembered hearing the priest say that word. The boy didn't know what it meant, but he'd felt the definition of the word as Father had said it.

Desecration.

The plumber stepped from his shack again, doling out frowns to the passersby. Pindip didn't understand this man. He had a trade. He had income. He had a house *and* a shop to work from. What else was there to need? Why should the plumber be unhappy?

With one last spit into the street, the plumber retreated into his workshop. Pindip knew the place's exact layout. He'd spent more than one night in the shop, stamping every corner and crevice, every shelf and every tool into his memory.

It had been days since the attack. Some of the orphan boys, the ones who had forgotten how to live on their own, tried to stay at the church. Two died at the hands of the ruffians who'd murdered the priest.

Desecration.

Then the church had been ransacked. Pindip watched as the men knocked over the holy altar from where the priest gave his sermons. They kicked it over like a rotting log in the jungle.

Desecration.

They'd left no section of the church unplundered, rifling through files they could not read, tossing the bunk beds of the boys and girls who called the place home. They'd taken what few things belonged to Pindip; his blanket, a pillow so soft Pindip often imagined it a cloud high in the sky that was his alone to cherish, the knick-knacks he'd picked up over the years, now crushed under muddy boots. Everything gone now.

Desecration.

The coast was clear. He slipped from his hiding place, a tiny nook between a vegetable stall and a massage parlor frequented by visitors from the city. He'd been there for hours. His legs ached when he finally moved, but he didn't complain. He never complained.

Off he went to find another temporary place to lay his head, to think more on his predicament, to adjust the angles in his agile mind.

Off he went to think of his angel, to hope that his guardian would come soon.

CHAPTER SIXTEEN

D ays passed without another adventure, and Cal began a bizarre routine of boredom on the island. He was now allowed to roam the house without an escort. Wilcox even let him take Liberty down to the beach where she leaped in and out of the foamy surf, shaking herself off before the odd passerby, who'd in turn take Liberty up on an offer to chuck a well-gnawed tennis ball back out into the water.

She sat nudging Cal's hand as he gazed out over the azure ocean.

"Sorry, girl," he said, realizing he had the ball in his hand. He lobbed it out into the surf and Liberty took off like a cheetah. She crashed down, chomping into the ball. And when she returned her eyes were bright, a dog's smile, utterly happy with her lot in life.

Must be nice, he thought.

Then came the mental rebuke. Enough feeling sorry for himself. He'd had time to think on his lot in life. Not a bad gig really. Even in his current predicament, life could've been so much worse.

Wilcox had been the perfect host, cooking meals himself,

explaining to Cal where and how the children they'd saved would be cared for.

This led to questions about their other exploits, about which Wilcox was surprisingly, even charmingly candid.

Cal remembered one such conversation they'd had at lunch the day before over omelets prepared in the French style.

"Imagine a currency that no government can regulate," Wilcox said. "Anyone can buy it, from a pedant in Bangladesh to an oil tycoon in Texas. No rules. Completely safe."

"Safe? Really? What do you call those goons raiding the computer geek's house?"

Wilcox shrugged. "Like anything, Cal, currency, no matter the kind, will always be a target. For now, it's a good way to make some money. A lot of it really."

"How much is a lot in your estimate?"

"Let's put it this way. The haul we made the other day? That was about twenty."

Cal slowed his chewing. "Twenty what?"

Wilcox grinned around his eggs. "Come on, Cal." He pointed to his mouth with his fork. "Look at this smile. Only millions can do that."

"I can't believe you don't feel a shred of remorse for the extortion."

"I can't believe you do," said Wilcox. "He's a smart kid. He'll make more."

And that was it. Cut and dry. Black and white. There was no hesitation in Wilcox's choices. That along with his perfect hosting duties were the only patterns Cal could discern in Wilcox's actions. In a way, he was some twisted Robin Hood, stealing from the rich to give to himself in order to help the poor and unfortunate. But did that make it right? It was still stealing. It was still breaking the law.

It was still Wilcox.

Liberty dropped the soaking tennis ball on the sand and Cal picked it up, quick to throw it mindlessly back in the ebbing tide. Out went the dog again, tireless in her pursuit of the ball, fearless.

AN HOUR LATER, now shaved and showered, Cal and Liberty joined Wilcox on the back patio for lunch. Wilcox was dressed in his usual, bright board shorts and a matching t-shirt that would've made a skate boarder jealous.

"Lunch is served," said Wilcox, motioning for Cal to take a seat. "And I got something special for you, girl." He knelt on the ground and produced something from behind his back. A bone, thick and full of marrow.

Her tail kicking into overdrive, Liberty stepped forward and eagerly took the bone from Wilcox.

When he reached out to pet the dog, she let out a growl and slipped back to Cal's side.

Atta girl.

"You'll come around," Wilcox said, unperturbed. "They all do."

"It's okay," Cal said with a reassuring pat on the dog's head. "Go on."

Liberty eyed Wilcox and went back to the bone.

"Getting the message?" said Cal.

"What message?"

"You can feed them well, but that doesn't automatically make them your friend."

"Very funny."

"Speaking of, what's for lunch?" Cal asked, taking his customary seat facing the beach, the seat he'd assumed at their first lunch together. It had been a conscious choice. Better to see someone coming. But Wilcox never worried about such things. On the rare occasion that they went into town for a meal, he barely took a second look around, even while Cal continued his casual scan of their surroundings.

"Kept it simple today. BLTs," Wilcox said, settling into his chair.

The bacon was thick, tomatoes juicy, and bread just perfectly toasted.

Too perfect.

That was Wilcox's ace. Ease the tension, create diversions — be they culinary or geographical — all in the effort to create the grand illusion of two old friends on an island vacation. Once again, Cal had been lulled into complacency.

Shake that off.

"When are you going to tell me what we're doing here?"

Wilcox looked up. Cutting through the bullshit had worked. "I thought that was obvious. Besides, we're leaving in an hour."

Cal's skin prickled at the proclamation, like a general had just sounded the warning bell for battle.

Wilcox finished his sandwich, took a long drink of fresh-squeezed orange juice, and leaned back to let the sunlight cast over his upper body.

"This island does funny things to your brain. Makes you lose all cares, don't you think?"

Cal shook his head. There he went again, just on the edge of reading Cal's mind.

"So, where are we going?"

"You'll see."

"At least tell me what we're doing."

Wilcox shook his head, still angled at the sun. "That'll spoil the surprise." He then looked at Cal, a shit-eating grin plastered across his face. "Tell me, what fun would that be?"

CHAPTER SEVENTEEN

Two flights and a day and half later, the private plane let the three travelers off at a remote airport on the outskirts of Copenhagen. The stiff wind blew in, making Cal hitch up his collar.

Wilcox had a private word with the pilot and then came out the door to meet Cal and Liberty.

"Well, here we are. Wonderful, wonderful Copenhagen. What do you think?"

"Nice runway," Cal said, unamused.

They didn't wait long. As was now custom, a blacked-out Lincoln pulled up minutes after the plane left. Not a word from the driver, just a nod. Everything taken care of.

How did Wilcox find the time to do it? Wilcox was almost always around, rarely on his phone, and more attentive to his guest than the goings-on of the world around him. Maybe he'd planned it months in advance. Who knew.

THE BOUTIQUE HOTEL was tucked in a quaint corner of Copenhagen. The staff was curt but welcoming in the way of the Nordic caste. Two double beds took up the majority of the space in the room, which had a curious art deco chair in the corner where there was no real practical space for it. Liberty jumped on the bed closest to the window and plopped down.

"I guess that one's yours," Wilcox said.

"Get down, girl," Cal said with a sigh.

Liberty hopped down from her perch, tail wagging expectantly. She'd been unusually calm on the flight. Like Cal, it seemed that the dog was getting used to Wilcox.

The words crept into Cal's subconscious. Be alert. The punchline's coming.

"Unpack if you want," Wilcox said. "We're leaving in five minutes."

On to the next adventure.

THEIR WALK WENT from minutes to hours. Wilcox described the city like he'd lived there since childhood. He really did have a gift for storytelling, always weaving some interesting tidbit of a ruling family's downfall or the rise of a figure of the day into the tapestry of his tale.

"And here we are," Wilcox announced.

Cal looked all around. They'd made their way into a seedy part of the industrial section of the city.

"Am I supposed to be impressed?"

"Are you?"

Liberty was the one to answer with a growl, apparently feeling her master's annoyance as well.

"Stop with the games. What are we doing here?"

Wilcox held up a finger like he was testing for rain. He stayed that way for a few beats, and then Cal heard it. The telltale sound of an approaching helicopter. The thumping grew louder until finally they saw the bird flying in.

"You ready?" Wilcox said.

"For what?"

"When was the last time you fast-roped?"

"You're kidding right?" He motioned to the casual business attire both men were wearing.

"Me, kid? Never." Shit-eating grin.

The helicopter settled fifty feet away, sending a cascade of loose gravel in all direction. Wilcox walked toward the bird, shoving any forthcoming questions right back down Cal's throat.

Onboard, a box of gear to put on over their clothes – a pack for each – and pair of boots.

"For the drop," said Wilcox.

"I get it," said Cal, fully understanding the basic rule that wearing a pair of Florsheim loafers down a rope at high speed would tear the things, no matter how well-crafted, right down through the sole.

Cal changed his shoes while Wilcox opened a waterproof box the size of a case of beer. Two pistols came out first, suppressors next along with extra magazines already loaded. Cal put a hand out for one of the weapons.

Wilcox shook his head. "When we get on the ground," he said over the roar of rotors.

If Wilcox lived in constant fear of Cal, he certainly knew how to hide it. But there was no denying that Cal, given the opportunity, would be the soldier he was. He could do it right now, he thought, reach over and wrestle one of the weapons away from Wilcox, insert the magazine, load a round into the chamber and shoot.

But that's not what he did. Instead he just nodded and followed the plan dutifully. Like the good soldier that he was.

· · ·

THE ROPE WENT out the open hatch and tumbled down into empty space. Trees below, as far as the eye could see. Through the canopy then.

Liberty was strapped to Cal and currently sitting in his lap. He'd never used one of those K9 rigs used by elite K9 units, and while Liberty had squirmed a bit getting strapped in, she now sat quietly, like she fully understood the gravity of the coming situation. Gravity. Now *there* was a word to describe what awaited them.

Wilcox slapped Cal on the back. "Ready?"

He didn't wait for a response, just grabbed the rope and sped down, wisps of smoke rising from the gloves as he slid down.

Cal adjusted his own gloves. "Here we go, girl."

And out they went, following the mad man once again.

CHAPTER EIGHTEEN

The forest was of a kind Cal had never experienced. That old air again, like the trees had seen the coming and going of a millennium and barely rustled a leaf. Given another time, he could've sat there for days, just walking from tree to tree trying to absorb their wisdom.

No time for that now. He met Wilcox on the ground who was in a crouch, scanning the area, weapon out.

Once Liberty was untethered, she took a few steps and did her business.

Wilcox motioned to the dog. "She gonna be quiet?"

"If I tell her to."

"Good. Here." He handed Cal one of the pistols. "Before you get any ideas, you're gonna need me with you. Lots of bad guys out there. Don't let your bravado get in the way of staying alive."

Cal didn't need the warning. He'd already decided to let Wilcox live, at least for the time being. There was something in these little vignettes they were acting out. What was the point? What was the goal? Where was the end game?

"I got it. Which way do we go?"

Wilcox consulted his watch and motioned with his chin. "That a way."

"I assume I'm walking point."

Wilcox grinned, that teenage mischievousness bursting forth again. "Can't have you gunning for me yet."

THERE WERE TURNS every half hour or so. Sometimes they paralleled well-worn paths, other times they were hip deep in scrub. But the going was easy compared to what Cal was used to.

Liberty ran the front, flitting from side to side, always checking in every couple of minutes. She never needed direction, always seeming to know the way.

An hour and a half in, things changed. Cal found Liberty pointing, front leg raised, straight ahead. He bent down so he could get a better look at what she saw.

It took him a few seconds for his eyes to catch the movement. The figure was maybe seventy-five yards away, moving slowly, methodically.

"Good girl," he whispered.

Wilcox was with them now.

"Good work, pup," he said, passing a hand over Liberty's coat. She didn't flinch. "Okay, Cal. Ready to work?"

"Sure thing, Boss."

"Good. You keep lead. I assume she knows what she's doing, but we stay as quiet as we can. We make noise and the cavalry comes calling. Got it?"

Cal didn't think the question rated a response. Of course, he was going to be quiet. No warrior wails here. He did have a question, the obvious one.

"You mind telling me who they are before we ambush?"

For a moment Cal didn't think Wilcox was going to answer.

"Bad guys," he finally said, "the worst. I can't believe they made it this far."

"Why should I trust you? How do I know they're not security for the King of Sweden?"

"First, I like the King of Sweden. Second, I thought you'd know me by now. Bad guys. That's who I hunt."

"What about the Russian ambassador?"

"What about him?"

"Why did you kill him?"

"Um, excuse me," Wilcox said with impatience, "we don't have time for this. Tango number one is about to walk this way."

He was right. The man had turned, and it would only be a matter of moments before they were spotted. It wasn't like they were wearing camouflage.

"I want to know. Why did you kill the ambassador?"

Wilcox huffed, one of the few times Cal had seen him discomfited. "Why does it matter?"

"If you ask that, then you don't know me at all."

The man in the distance moved closer.

Wilcox had his pistol ready in one hand, and a blade had found its way into his other. "How about this," he said. "You tell me what you know about the ambassador."

"For starters, he was on the short list to take over the country. Patriotic, but a friend of the West. Good for reform. Anti-corruption. Everything we need in a leader of Russia."

The shake of Wilcox's head. "You, with all your connections."

"What?"

"You don't know anything."

"Then talk to me, smartass."

Tango was getting close. Thirty seconds, tops.

"I didn't want to get into this now, but it seems that you aren't going to give me a choice." Wilcox inhaled, still focused at the man moving their way. "That ambassador, your pinnacle of change, he was the worst of them. All that goody-two-shoes crap, it was a front."

"What did he do?"

"What didn't he do? Smuggling. Trafficking. Laundering. Nuclear proliferation."

"Bullshit."

Wilcox's eyes were cold steel. "Time to buck up, Cal. I'm surprised at your naïveté. You of all people should know that the world isn't what it seems."

"But—"

"He lied to you."

The statement set Cal back. Wilcox had read his mind again. "Who lied?"

Five seconds until contact.

"No time."

"Tell me."

Another annoyed huff from Wilcox's mouth. "President Zimmer, you idiot. He's been lying to you the whole time."

That's when the shooting started.

CHAPTER NINETEEN

Wilcox took down the first guy with a single shot. Forehead dimple.

"Come on." Wilcox was already running, Liberty close on his heels.

Zimmer? What was Wilcox talking about?

No time for that now.

Targets popped up in Cal's field of vision, dark and roving. Patrols who hadn't heard the muffled fall of their comrade.

Cal was maybe ten strides behind Wilcox. He could've done it. He could've ended it all right then and there. Two bullets to the back of the head. Or maybe a shot to each leg and he could get all the answers he needed.

But here it was, the tsunami swallowing Cal up in its wake. No diverging from the path. On he ran, footfalls as light as his two companions. He actually saw Wilcox grin at the specter that was Liberty as she tracked their next target. She did not hesitate. Six feet from the next man, who'd swiveled to the noise in the underbrush, she leaped, a long jump, like an Olympian going for distance before hitting the sand.

The dog's aim was perfect, her mouth clamping down on the

man's jugular, jaw clenching even as Wilcox came up behind and put two shots into the man. Liberty cradled the corpse to the ground.

Man and beast exchanged a satisfied look. Cal couldn't help but feel the coursing jealousy, black and biting in his veins.

He overtook Wilcox, the dog now in tow.

He felt it, the tug, the pull, the universal enticement of the kill. Not for enjoyment. Not for fun. For the test of it, to show...

The undergrowth cleared now, like someone tended the forest every morning with a rake. Liberty paced her master, already reading his mind, the duo pursuing their next target without a word, without a thought.

It was so easy. So clean. So efficient. Like the ancient hunter she was, Liberty slowed and allowed Cal his chance. Their next target turned just in time. Two shots to the chest and one to the head. They ran on past.

Too much noise, Cal thought, his mind detached, his breathing coming in perfect intervals, a killing athlete.

Another, then another. On they went, Wilcox somewhere behind them. Sometimes Liberty would take the lead, sometimes Cal. They were in sync; two killers, primordial and ravenous for blood, but a clockwork machine of death nonetheless.

By the time they took down their sixth target, the humanity in Cal returned.

Slow down.

Liberty stiff-sniffed, rising on her back legs to look further through the canopy. She stopped, pointing again.

"You found it," Wilcox said, panting behind them. "Nice moves, by the way. Very smooth."

Cal stared ahead, doing his best to digest what had just taken place. He'd killed. Knowingly and perfectly, he'd killed. Who were the men who were now pouring their blood onto the manicured forest floor?

No clue. Why didn't that matter?

The answer lay within him, somewhere. As sure as his veins burned with adrenaline, he knew Wilcox had told the truth, that the men who lay dead had been protecting some evil entity that needed to be erased from the earth.

"Come on. Our host is waiting."

Liberty followed Wilcox to the structure up ahead, a building that looked to be the same age as the forest, with high sweeping windows and wood paneling that matched its surroundings. It reminded Cal of the perfect tree house, something he would've loved as a kid.

No more targets. Liberty confirmed that fact by remaining focused straight ahead.

The place had no front lawn. It was just the woods and then the house, as if the place had been grown there, bioengineered by sentient flora.

Cal pointed to a camera mounted under an eave.

"They're off," Wilcox answered absentmindedly. "Let's get this over with."

Something in his voice. Regret. Like a reluctant cop arresting his beloved brother.

The front door, heavy and laden with wood at least three inches thick, opened without a care. Wilcox pushed his way in. Liberty and Cal a moment later.

The inside of the place was nothing like the exterior. All high-vaulted ceiling and clean Nordic wood, the smell of pine and something cooking in the kitchen. Fish, maybe.

And there, sitting on the couch holding a glass of white wine, was a man Cal recognized instantly. He was a man most of the world knew, a savior to some, a celebrity to others. A man of substance and outreach. A man who'd spent his near-sixty years gracing the world with his presence.

Cal had met the man before, found him to be congenial,

competent and a man of his word. Or at least that's what he had thought.

The man reached out and placed his glass on the coffee table, taking his time as he stretched back out on the couch.

And with a tone that rang of mild curiosity he asked, "Is it too late to beg for my life?"

Ervin Hill, the United States Secretary of State, a one-time candidate for the presidency, war hero and former actor, shifted his gaze from Wilcox to Cal. There was no uneasiness there, just calm acceptance.

CHAPTER TWENTY

CAL'S JOURNAL

What would you think if you walked into a room with a gun, hellbent on killing a bad man, a man whose disappearance would help the world in innumerable ways?

Now, what if the man sitting in that room was a man you knew, someone you'd met and respected? How would that change things?

My life hasn't been easy. Whose has? Life isn't easy and that's okay. If it were, we'd all be lazy slobs obsessed with our own moral righteousness.

I've come to understand, through too much death and darkness, that there are consequences to everything. Take my chosen profession as an example. I was a reluctant participant at first. I didn't want to follow in my father's footsteps. SSI was his company not mine. It was something he built brick by brick, through good times and bad. SSI was his baby.

Maybe that's why it was so easy to leave.

Who am I kidding? Leaving SSI wasn't easy, but it was the right thing to do.

So then I move on and we form The Jefferson Group. Our mission was simple, find bad guys and kill them or bring them to justice before they could do harm to our country. Simple, right?

Killing is never simple. Killing is often layered with so many levels of truth and fable. Sometimes it's hard to pull the fiction from what's real.

There I go. Rambling again.

Back to the man in the room.

Would you kill a man you knew?

I would.

Why?

If I thought he was a good moral man, and then I found out that he was nothing of the kind, there would be no hesitation in my trigger pull. A bullet for justice.

Justice.

How much time have I spent thinking about that word? A word so many in earth's long history have twisted to their own games of power.

Justice.

So yeah, I stood in a room with a man I knew, and I knew I had to kill him. Something in me pushed to pull the trigger, to wipe the stain of his existence from the flesh of the world. Easy. One and done.

How had I come to that point? How had I come to trust Wilcox, the Robin Hood of the downcast?

I can't explain it.

You had to be there. How many times have I heard that?

"Why did you drop a bomb on a hospital, Captain?"

"You had to be there, sir."

"Why did you shoot that boy climbing in the window, Sergeant?"

"You had to be there, Lieutenant."

Perspective. Time.

How can I explain it? I can't. It just is. So there you go.

It just is.

CHAPTER TWENTY-ONE

"Gentlemen," said Ervin Hill, "I'm sure it's not too late to do something about your predicament."

The Secretary of State was suave in every way. But Cal saw it, the edge of nerves. The slightly flared nose of indignation. The dilated pupils of fear. A man conflicted. A man facing the barrel of a weapon.

"We're way past that, Mr. Secretary," said Wilcox. "Have you had a pleasant stay, Mr. Secretary? Did you enjoy Copenhagen?"

A sneer and a smile. "Why don't you cut the crap, pal. Tell me what you want and I'm sure our government will pay."

"You're humping the wrong leg, Mr. Secretary. We're not here for money."

"Then what do you want?"

"Tell him, Cal."

Cal stared at Wilcox. "Tell him what?"

Wilcox closed his eyes, shook his head. "Stupid me. Mr. Secretary, my good friend Cal here is a Marine, or, was a Marine. I never know what's the right thing to say after the commandant said there's no such thing as a former Marine."

Cal rolled his eyes.

"Okay, okay." Wilcox stepped close, placed his boot on top of their captive's knee. The man flinched. "Cal is a Marine. His best friend is another Marine named Daniel Briggs."

Daniel's name elicited confusion and then a dramatic change. Cal saw the beads of sweat pop up on Hill's forehead.

"I had nothing to do with that," he stammered. Cool gone.

"Liar."

"No, I promise... "

Wilcox's pistol came down in a swooping motion, slamming into the secretary's cheek. "Tell the truth, Mr. Secretary. Daniel Briggs fought and almost died for our country. Tell Cal why you soil the memory of his sacrifice, the memory of his spotter, and the memory of those brave, dead SEALS just by continuing to steal precious breath on Earth."

Cal stood frozen. Of course, he knew the story. Briggs on a support mission for a SEAL team. Insurgents appeared like ants out of an ant hill, swarming and screaming for death. He shot too many to count. All the SEALs died and Briggs spent a miserable handful of days cradling his dead spotter, his best friend, until friendly troops found him. The then American president would later request the honor of bestowing the Medal of Honor on the brave Marine. Briggs didn't want it. He refused. The days and years after that horrific mistake had plagued Daniel for a long journey.

"Come on, Mr. Secretary. I've never seen you at a loss for words."

The secretary's mouth opened and closed. No words. No explanation. Just cold realization.

Wilcox leaned forward, adding more weight to the pressed knee, and pressed his pistol to the man's forehead. "Speak, Mr. Secretary. Cal and his friend deserve the truth."

Eyes flitting from one captor to another. The composed politician turned crumbling man.

"I don't... I didn't."

The pistol struck again. A pained gasp from the man on the couch.

"I've got all day, Mr. Secretary. I'll beat you until you're nothing but a stain on that couch. But I won't let you die. No. My friend deserves the truth. Briggs deserves the truth. The world deserves the truth, the admission of your treachery."

"Fine, fine." The secretary avoided Cal's eyes when he said, "You're Zimmer's friend. I remember you now."

It took a good long minute for the secretary to compose himself. Wilcox eased off the knee, even stepped back when the man started to speak.

"It was a long time ago. I was new to the game. They told me what to expect, but... well, you never really know until you see it yourself." Silence. A heavy breath. "I'd never been to a war zone. Hell, I'd never really seen destruction like that... death everywhere. Body bags and bloody bandages. It haunted me as I tried to do my job. I tried to learn on the fly, for the sake of our nation. I still drank in those days."

Cal pointed to the now-empty wine glass. "I guess that was strawberry Quik?"

Hill's eyes met Cal's and then looked away just as quickly. "I meant I drank *too much*. They would bring a mobile bar in at nights, for visiting dignitaries to let off steam. Everyone was there, from presidents to lowly congressmen like yours truly. We mingled, discussed the horror we'd seen, all the while trying to drink away the memory of those troops. Their bloodshot eyes, their thousand-yard stares. They were the heroes. Not the rest of us. We were just pathetic, gin-soaked observers. What good our visits did I'll never know."

"You're avoiding the issue, Mr. Secretary," said Wilcox.

"Fine, fine." Another deep breath and a moistening of the lips, as his eyes glazed back to the past. "There was one truly horrible day—I say horrible and you're probably laughing inside. I know what you've seen. It's Stokes, isn't it?"

Cal stepped forward, gun in hand pointed right at the politician's head. "Keep talking."

The secretary leaned back, his torso inching up the couch as if trying to retreat into it.

"Easy, easy. It was a bad day. I drank more than I should have. They brought girls, women from villages. Not little boys or girls. Nothing like that. I never did that. Some did. It was disgusting. But we were there to do a job."

Cal's pistol struck with more force than he'd intended. The secretary bounced off the couch cushion. Cal put out a hand to stop him from toppling forward as he rebounded. The secretary's eyes were wide and tearing when Cal's hard glare locked in.

"Keep going, Mr. Secretary."

All the politician could do now was nod. Cal slapped him with the back of his hand. "Talk."

The secretary's hands were up, trying to shield his face. Blood trickled form his temple and the right corner of his mouth. A man physically and emotionally wrecked.

"I drank too much. I laid with a girl. I don't even remember what she looked like. When I woke up in the morning she was gone. I didn't know what I'd done—"

Cal grabbed the front of the man's collar, his knuckles white and quivering. "What did you do?"

"I told her... I told her about the mission. I told her why we were there. It's my fault. I was the one who got those poor boys killed."

CHAPTER TWENTY-TWO

Shock. Pure, unadulterated, basic human shock. Like someone had reached inside Cal's chest and gripped his heart, willed it to stop.

He staggered back two steps.

"I'm sorry." The politician blubbered uncontrollably like a child.

Cal shook his head, took another two steps back.

Daniel Briggs. He was one of the most decent, solid, genuine people Cal had ever met. A best friend in every sense of the word. He had no qualms about coming to a brother's aid. He didn't walk, he flew, the avenging angel always close by.

And that man, the one sitting on the couch that seemed like he was a football field length away from Cal now, he was the one who'd plunged Daniel into years of pain, a darkness so complete that it had almost consumed him.

What am I supposed to do?

What would Daniel do?

"Kill him," bade Wilcox's voice, far and coaxing.

Cal looked over at him. There was no smile, no "I got you"

jeering. The shit-eating grin was gone, replaced by the granite look of cold truth.

"Please don't," the secretary held out his hands, and fell to his knees. The penitent man.

What would Daniel do?

All those men lost, and why? Because this asshole couldn't keep his mouth shut in front of some sweet-smelling whore, couldn't stay away from the bottle, couldn't control his urges.

Cal closed his eyes, willed a breath in, a breath out.

When he opened his eyes, they were still there, still standing in the idyllic cabin set in the deep woods, a place he would've loved to stay given different circumstances.

The secretary scrambled forward on all fours. At this sight, Liberty jumped out front, growling in a way Cal had never seen. Did she understand what had just transpired? Could she sense the pit of evil inside humans like this?

The secretary froze at the sight of her, tears dripping onto the hardwood floor.

"He's yours, Cal," Wilcox said icily. "Do it for them, for the men who didn't deserve to die."

"Is this why you brought me here?"

Wilcox turned his hard gaze to him. "Part of the reason."

"And what's the rest of it?"

Wilcox shook his head slowly, as if measuring time with it. "Now is not the time." He motioned to the man on the floor, now guarded by the snarling Liberty and her raised hackles.

"When is the time?"

"I'll tell you when. Do it. Now. For the men. For *Daniel*."

"Screw you. Tell me!"

As if in answer, Wilcox huffed, turned, and shot the Secretary of State four times in rapid succession. Ervin Hill's body stiffened, relaxed, and fell over. Dead.

Wilcox turned and looked at Cal. "You're no fun, you know that?"

He turned on his heel and left through the front door.

CHAPTER TWENTY-THREE

The men came in the night, led by the one who'd choked the priest to death. Three were Filipino, men Pindip knew to be associated with the local criminal underground.

The others he didn't recognize, and it wasn't because of the staggering light. They were light-skinned. Americans? Australians?

Two of them whispered to each other.

Pindip recognized the bits and pieces of the language. *Russian.*

When you scrounged for life, scraps of foreign languages helped almost as much as food. Russians had come to his village before, paraded in like occupying soldiers, like they owned all of the Philippines.

Pindip always knew he had to be a little more careful around such men. Brutality wafted off of them like cologne. And the men he watched now were no different. Two wore beards, big bushy things like the boy had never seen.

One of the Russians said something to the murderer, pushed him forward. Three Filipinos against seven Russians. No match, although Pindip wished the murderer would press the foreigners. Then they would strangle him, like he'd strangled poor Father Francis.

They entered a bar in a low hovel three blocks from the deserted church.

He knew he was taking a chance by stalking them, but he had to. It couldn't be coincidence that the Russians were here. He'd prayed and prayed for God to bring his angel, Matthew. He'd been unfamiliar – as he was now – of God's mysteries. Father Francis had told him that was a good thing. God's love was a place of joy, and such joy burned away sadness and pain. And so, the boy prayed. When he finished, he slipped from the roof and skirted the long way around, finally ending up behind the seedy bar. Filipino rap music thumped through ancient speakers inside.

The back door was locked – probably bolted tight from the inside.

He stepped into a blanket of shadow and said another prayer.

Please, God, let me see, let me hear.

He opened his eyes. And his smile consumed half his face, and he ambled over to the metal wall and the small hole that let out the barest hint of light.

THE MEN INSIDE WERE SEPARATED, dark skin on one side of the table and white on the opposing side. The Russians drank and spoke in their native tongue, laughing like they were on holiday.

The natives were another case entirely. They sat staring, sipping on beers that didn't seem to have any effect on their fidgeting. Minutes passed, then a half hour.

Maybe this was nothing. Maybe it was a meeting between mismatched friends.

No. It was impossible. The level of discomfort on the Filipino side was obvious.

Finally, with a lift of his mug and a downing of his beer, the head Russian, a man with impressive biceps and crew cut blonde hair, began the real conversation.

"When was the last time you saw him?" the Russian asked the Filipino head thug.

"I... we haven't."

"That is not what you told my employer."

"I never said..."

"Shut your mouth, dog." The massive Russian turned to his companions. On each of their faces was a look Pindip had seen many times in his short life, though it was a look that stretched back thousands of years: a ravenous hunger for violence.

"You see, friends?" he continued, "We come to their pitiful country, their haven of mongrels, and what do they do? They lie to us! They waste our time. I ask, what does one do with a pack of lying dogs?"

"No, please!" the Filipino said, raising his hands in the air, spilling half his beer on his head in the process.

"Put your hands down," the Russian said, dragging out every syllable.

The hands went down. Beer dripped from the Filipino's nose onto his chest.

The seconds ticked by and no one moved. The music kept thumping and beer kept dripping, but everything else stood still – a time warp in the middle of the Philippines.

"This man," said the Russian, "this American. What did he look like?"

The beer-covered thug sputtered, "I told you I... we, never saw him."

"Then how do you know that he's an American?"

"The children," said the man, wiping his dripping nose with his sleeve, "they told us."

"The orphans?"

"Yes."

"And where are they now, the orphans."

"Scattered. Living under bridges and inside of alleys."

The Russian snorted. "It will make them stronger. You know that, don't you? They'll grow up, become stronger. And then they will come for you and your friends." He laughed straight up at the ceiling. "Oh, how I wish I could be here to see that day!"

The rest of the Russians joined in on the raucous laughter. Two of them clinked beer glasses.

The leader picked his phone off the table, pecked at it for a few moments, then held it up for the Filipino to see.

"Is this him?"

Pindip adjusted so he could get a better look. Thanks to his keen eyesight he was able to zero in. It wasn't the angel Matthew.

"I tell you I don't know."

"What about this one?" The Russian flipped to another picture. Another Pindip didn't recognize. "And this one?" The Filipino shook his head, his body shaking involuntarily, his legs quivering.

"Please, I tell you I don't know."

"What good are you, dog? Tell me why we shouldn't kill you and force your filthy friends to eat your entrails. We can do that, you know. We did it in Afghanistan. We did it in Chechnya. You've never tasted power until you've made comrades eat one of their own. Maybe with a little of your country's famous *bagoóng* for taste." He looked over his shoulder towards the bar. "Tell me, bartender, do you have any *bagoóng*?"

"No, please!" the head thug screamed. He went to raise his hands but thought better of it. He seemed to compose himself and then he spoke, his voice shaking as badly as his legs. "There was a boy, the one who tried to help the priest. He know who the American is."

Pindip's stomach clenched.

"Yes, the boy," one of the other Filipinos said enthusiastically. "What was his name?"

The outnumbered trio bobbed their heads like monkeys, trying to come up with the answer.

"*Pindip*," the third man said. "That is it. Pindip. We will find him for you and he will help you find the American."

"For a price," the head thug dared to say.

The Russian delegation glared for a long minute.

"Very well, bring us this boy and we will pay..." He leaned in. "With your lives. We'll let you keep them."

Pindip backed away from the hole in the wall. His legs felt like they couldn't move him more than an inch a minute. They'd remembered. They knew who he was. All it would take was threatening some shopkeepers or slapping around some house-wives and they would find out enough information to locate him.

He thought about leaving. He could head to another town, maybe the city. He could get lost there. Start a new life.

No. That wouldn't do, he thought. His angel was coming. Matthew would help.

And besides, if Matthew did come, someone had to warn him about these men who were after him. It didn't take Pindip more than a breath to come to the decision. He would stay. He would hide. He would wait.

With a renewed sense of courage, he spun on his heel, his legs working away, ready to speed him off to one of his many hiding spaces. He needed time to think, time to plan.

He didn't make it more than a single step before he ran straight into the protruding belly of a large man.

"What are you doing out here, boy?" the man said, his voice not much more than a slur. He reeked of sweat and foulness.

"I was..." Pindip looked all around. "Peeing."

"Then why were you looking through that hole? I use that

hole too, you know, to watch the girls they bring from the villages when foreigners come. I was just in there. There aren't any girls."

Pindip tried to get around the man but a meaty hand clamped down on one shoulder, pinning the boy in place.

"Where do you think you're going?"

"Home. My mo..."

"You know something? I think you were spying. I think someone in there would like to know that you were spying. Maybe those rude Russians."

He reached down with another hand and hoisted Pindip over his shoulder. The boy squirmed but it was no use. They were moving now, around the building towards the front door.

The boy kicked and punched, which only seemed to amuse the man. He went at the man with his teeth, trying to tear his way to freedom. The man appeared to enjoy that too, digging his filthy nails into the boy's legs with great merriment.

But by the time they'd reentered the stinking bar, there was no more amusement, and Pindip was tossed to the ground like a heavy sack.

He looked up, straight into the eyes of the hulking Russian.

CHAPTER TWENTY-FOUR

CAL'S JOURNAL

I've had time to think about it. Hell, I knew the answer before we'd even left Copenhagen.

I felt zero point zero guilt for Hill's death. None. Nada.

Maybe that's because I didn't do it. It was Wilcox. He did it without the slightest hesitation. His disappointment with me didn't last long either. It wasn't even an hour before he was chatting away like we'd just been on a bus tour of the city.

I only half listened, still digesting what had happened in the woods. The kill. The confrontation. The revelation.

What would Daniel think when I told him?

Part of me knew that he'd already moved on from that tragic story. He'd put it behind him like a page in a history book he'd never look at again.

But not me. I'd never been that way. I could turn the page but I always went back. Call it shame, or call it self-punishment, why did I always look back?

I thought I'd come to a place in my life where I controlled everything. I controlled what I put in my body. I controlled the decisions I made. I controlled the people I surround myself with. But did I really?

Here I am with Wilcox, playing along like some twisted play. I don't know why I'm here. I don't know what he wants from me. It's like he's waiting for something. He wanted me to kill that bastard in the woods. He wanted me to lash out. But why? What was it he wants?

Now back to me. I left my friends against their advice. I flew into the heart of Satan, and for what? For the truth? What truth? For answers? What answers do I need?

That's the thing. I don't know. That cave did something to me. I don't know what it was, but it cut me in a place I can't see. Like there's a Pandora's box in my chest just waiting to be opened. But what's inside the box? What's inside me?

So I take one day at a time, waiting, wanting.

I get glimpses of Diane in my memories. The good times and the bad. I bathe myself in the bad while trying to wash away the good. And why do I do that? Why do I wallow in filth when I should be celebrating the joy?

Maybe it's because I've forgotten what joy feels like.

CHAPTER TWENTY-FIVE

"You work hard, Cal. You take care of your men. That's how you win."

Cal's father stepped out of the scene, like a shadow flowing away in a blink of a second.

"But, Dad..."

The specter was gone and Cal had so many questions. He was a kid again, a teenager with his father the pinnacle of light and goodness. The one to look up to.

"Dad!" Cal screamed, but the scream sounded muffled like he'd yelled into a muffled pit of nothingness.

No response. No sage words. He was gone.

He felt the cold on his cheek first, like water dripping down a wall that he'd pressed his face to. Cal recoiled. He was in the cave again sucking precious water from the cave wall. The frozen fear reared, sinking deep into his chest, numbing in a way he'd never forget.

The feeling came again, cool against the cheek, more insistent now. He tried to move away, tried to push it away, but it stayed.

Cal's eyes shot open and he was looking straight into Liberty's almond eyes. She'd been pressing her cold snout against his face.

Cal exhaled and closed his eyes pressing the memories from his brain like an orange squeezed for its juice.

"Sorry, girl. Was I talking in my sleep?"

Liberty set her face right next to his. She let out a low whine.

"It's okay. Come on, let me take you out."

Normally she would've spun circles, but this time she just sat there staring at him. Judging or protecting?

WHEN LIBERTY WAS DONE RELIEVING herself, and taking a sniff around the perimeter of the beach house, the pair went back inside. The smell of bacon and eggs greeting them. Wilcox was in the kitchen playing chef again.

"Good morning," he said, not looking up from where he was stirring eggs with the grace of an orchestra leader. "Sleep well?"

Cal never knew how to answer. At least he was past the "grab a fork and stab Wilcox in the jugular" mindset.

"Slept fine."

"Me too. Like a baby. You know, I always sleep well, but damn do I kick into high REM when I've just finished a good mission. Same with you?"

"Sure."

Wilcox shook his head and chuckled. "Man, you sure are articulate when you wanna be. Hey, why don't you turn on the television? I wanna see what the weather's gonna be like today."

"You know, you can just look at your phone."

Wilcox looked up, all business. "Turn on the damn TV, Cal."

Cal turned on the wall-mounted TV and flipped to the news. There before him was the face of the man they'd visited, and killed, the day before.

"Secretary of State Hill was killed in a tragic plane crash yesterday outside Copenhagen. The White House is still investigating the exact details of the crash, but we have had word that

President Zimmer is on his way to deliver his condolences in person."

Wilcox laughed behind Cal.

Cal gritted his teeth at the sound and turned toward its source. "What the hell is so funny?"

"Your buddy, Zimmer. He's wasting his time. No sense mourning a piece of crap like Ervin Hill."

"He doesn't know what Hill did."

"Oh no?"

"What else do you know, Wilcox?"

Wilcox served breakfast on two plates, and after a thought, gave a single piece of bacon to Liberty who took it gratefully.

The grin returned. "Ah, I'm just messing with you. Zimmer is clueless as ever. But you should've seen the look on your face just now. You really should work on controlling your temper, Cal. It's no good for a person in our line of work."

"Yeah? What line of work is that? Murder?"

Wilcox sat down, took a bite of bacon followed by a long drink of orange juice. He sucked his teeth for a moment and said, "You think that's what this is? I think you need to look up the definition of murder, my friend. Sit down. The eggs are getting cold. I put a splash of sweet cream in them. They're really delicious."

"Enough. Tell me what the hell I'm doing here other than being witness to your insanity."

Wilcox sat his fork down mid-slice into his eggs. "You think I'm crazy?"

"What if I do? Are you going to kill me too?"

"If I wanted you dead, you'd be dead."

"You do want me dead. So do it."

Wilcox shook his head, picking up his fork and a scoop of scrambled eggs. "You know what's wrong with you, Cal? You've been playing with politicians too long. They've jumbled your perspective. You can't see right from wrong anymore, and what's more, they've got you convinced that *they're* the ones you should listen to. I've got news for you, pal. The boys in Washington are just as dumb as your average tree stump. You've been indoctrinated into their cult."

Cal was still standing, fists clenched at his side. "You keep saying you know me. You have no idea who I am or what I believe in."

Wilcox ate his bite of eggs and then pointed his fork at Cal. "I know you're a good man, Charlie Brown. That's why I picked you. All you need is a little..." he waved his fork in the air, "...tweaking."

He went back to attacking his eggs.

"What do you want from me, Wilcox?"

"Right now I want you to pass the salt. I tend to underseason when I'm cooking for someone else. It's a terrible habit." He looked at Cal, that unrelenting smirk on his face. "I want you to live up to your potential."

"What the hell does that mean?"

"In the words of Louis Armstrong, 'If you has ta ask, you'll never know.'"

Cal slammed a fist onto the table. "I'm not your goddamn student!"

Wilcox, unfazed by the sudden display, nevertheless looked like he'd just been slapped. "After everything I've done for you."

"You've done both jack and shit for me."

The fork settled onto the plate and Wilcox took a deep breath in then out.

"I thought you would've figured it out sooner rather than later. That's on me, I guess." He took another deep breath, thinking. "Look, you're right. I should've been more upfront. I don't like riddles either. You want to know what this is all about. Well, I'm serious when I say it's about getting you to your full potential, Cal."

"Thank you again, sensei. What the hell does that even mean?"

"The cave, this trip – they were all part of your journey."

"My journey?"

Wilcox picked up his fork again. It hovered over his plate looping in circles. "Listen, don't freak out on me. But I want you to tell me something. Tell me how you felt when they pulled you from the mountain."

Cal didn't think he was going to respond. He'd had enough of the mind games. But something, maybe it was the memory of his father in his dream, pushed him to answer.

"I felt... numb, dead inside."

"And why do you think that was?"

"I don't know."

"Sure you do."

"I don't."

"I'm sure your Doc Higgins would disagree. He's a pretty sharp guy. I'd like to meet him some day. At any rate, what does *he* say about the way you felt?"

"He said it was natural to feel the way I did, what with, well the file."

"The file about your dad."

Cal had read that file over and over again. He saw it in his sleep. The words came unbidden at the most random times.

"Yes. The one about my dad." Then, to his own complete surprise, he asked the question he'd been longing to ask since the first second he'd opened the file. "Was it real?"

Another bite of eggs. Another sip of orange. "What do you think, Cal?"

He would've jumped over the table if Liberty hadn't nudged his leg. She must've sensed his unease.

Wilcox sensed it too. "Fine," he said impatiently. "Yes. Of course it was real."

Even though Cal had known the answer, it still sent a jolt of sorrow spiking through him. His father. His hero. A liar. A cheat.

"I don't understand." Cal's words sounded distant, like someone had uttered them in a dream, or beneath the crashing waves.

Wilcox leaned forward, his shirt almost touching what was left on his breakfast plate. "I'll make you a promise right here and now. I will never lie to you. I never have."

Cal looked up from his own plate, fixed a murderous stare on his captor.

"Funny line even from you. You killed your own father. Is that what you thought I would do?"

"Your dad was already dead."

The comment made him clamp his teeth to keep his emotions at bay. He couldn't let it out, not here, not now.

Wilcox's voice grew soft. "Think back to what you know about me. How would you describe me, in a nutshell?"

"Nutcase."

"Good one. And fair, if you didn't know me. But I thought you'd have a different insight by now."

"Murderer."

Wilcox grinned. "Isn't that what Dante West would say about you?"

He picked up his fork and ate with gusto. The appetite of the triumphant.

CHAPTER TWENTY-SIX

Frozen.

How long did he sit there, just frozen?

That name. That long-ago nemesis: Dante West.

He'd put the man out of his thoughts for obvious reasons. For Cal, that was the beginning. The beginning of his new life. The beginning of his troubles. The beginning of who he'd become.

Dante West. Gangster. Drug dealer. Dead by Cal's own hands.

Cal's voice came out in a grated snarl. "Tell me more of what you know about that."

"I know everything about you, Cal. Come on. I told you. Do you really think I couldn't figure out that little snippet of your life?"

"We covered it up."

"Yeah? Well, people talk, Cal. You should know that. You were a Marine. You know how scuttlebutt works. Do they still call it that in the military? Gossip is like a virus that seeps out and spreads whether you want it to or not. So, I found out about West. And no, I'm not bringing it up to make you reconsider your life choices. I'm no life coach, Cal."

"Then what the hell are you?"

Wilcox leaned back, spread his arms wide. "Let's say I'm bringing order back. What would that make me?"

Cal laughed. "You're kidding, right?"

"How is what I do different than what you did to West?"

"It's different."

"Bullshit. It's the same damn thing and you know it. When have I ever lifted a finger to harm an innocent? Go ahead, think about it."

"Your father."

Wilcox threw his head back in a roaring laugh. "You think he was innocent? God, you are a deluded little mousey, you know that? My father was a liar, a crook, a man who would do anything to see that his illegitimate son was happy. At least your dad had the balls to try and fix what he'd done wrong."

He let that thought settle for a long pause.

Cal saw his father now, the proud man with the sea bag strapped over his shoulder, home from war. In his mind's eye, Cal Stokes Sr., the great Marine colonel, dropped the duffel bag and snatched up his wife and twirled her around. His son stood to one side, a child on the cusp of his teenage years, uncertain whether to run to his father or stick out a hand for a shake.

His father answered the question for him after gently putting Cal's mother back down. He marched over to his son and lifted him up in a crushing bear hug.

Cal felt the tears running down his face, felt the warmth of his father's love, unconditional and there till the end. *I miss you, Dad*, he thought.

"He was my best friend."

Wilcox cocked his head to one side. "Of course he was. Do you think I would've brought you all this way if he wasn't?"

"I still don't get it." Cal spoke but he still held on to that image of his father. He could smell his aftershave, the beard just turning rough rubbing against his cheek. Quick inhale in. Slow exhale out. "You said..."

"I said I wanted to show you the truth. That's what I'm doing. Ervin Hill. The kids on the boat. Dante West. They're all tied together."

"How?"

"We can do something about each and every one. God, or whatever you believe in, gave us the power to do it."

Cal shook his head emphatically. "That still doesn't explain what I'm doing here."

Another pause. Another few breaths.

"That time you spent under the mountain, I had to see."

"See what, dammit?"

"That you could come out of it. I'd trashed your hero and you crumbled. But you're coming out of it now. Your dad was human, Cal. He's still a hero. Mention his name in the top echelons of government and they still bow their heads in heavy reverence. That was one mistake. One cock-up in a lifetime of doing the right thing."

"So, you brought me here to teach me that lesson? An email would've sufficed."

"I had to talk to you face to face."

"I'm done." Cal pushed himself from the table. "I'm through with your twisted morality and half-truths. Do whatever you want with your life, Wilcox. I'm going to live mine."

He was almost to the door when Wilcox spoke.

"I brought you here to recruit you."

Cal stopped and turned. "You can't be serious."

"Look at my face." Dead serious.

"What makes you think I would even entertain... no, you know what? Forget I asked. Forget I was even here. Shock me. Shoot me if you want. I'm leaving."

"What if I told you we could fix it all?"

"Doesn't matter."

"Yes it does and you know it. Besides, how could you go back to working for Zimmer now that you know he's been lying to you."

"You're a con man, Wilcox."

"Am I? Give me one week. One week and I'll show you everything. If at the end of that week you think I'm full of crap, leave."

"How do I know I can trust you?"

"Did you hear me, Cal? I may be the devil but I'll never lie to you."

Cal met the man's eyes. "The devil is the father of lies, you realize that, don't you?"

That grin again. "At least we understand each other."

CHAPTER TWENTY-SEVEN

P alm trees as far as the eye could see.

Spaceships flying to Mars and beyond.

Houses bigger than castles.

Images all. Memories. Dreams.

Pindip tried to keep his eyes shut. The pictures in his head kept him from the horror of reality.

Think about the movies, he told himself, his eyes pressed so hard that they squeezed tears.

A rustling at the door. Keys and then the stomp of oversized boots.

"Get up," the skinny Russian said, the one with breath like rotten onions.

Pindip stayed laying down, holding on to the images.

Palm trees.

Spaceships.

Houses. No, *mansions*. That's what they were called.

"I said get up, boy."

A hard boot nudged him in the side.

No faking now.

His eyes eased open. The man looming over him wore gym

shorts, boots and nothing else. He was covered in sweat, like he'd gone for a run in the summer heat.

"Get up if you want to eat."

The voice wasn't unkind. All business really. Bored.

The boy sat up and the man left. A look around the room revealed that nothing had changed overnight. Same room. No curtain. Sun trying to blast its way in through the plywood nailed over the only window in the room.

The room was bare except for the blanket they'd given him to sleep on. It had scratched at his skin the entire night. A boy of the streets, he knew a scratchy blanket was better than a bed of trash. At least this room was clean.

A sudden need to relieve himself sent him to his feet.

He knocked on the door as hard as he dared. They hadn't touched him, other than to load him into the truck on the way to his current predicament. They hadn't even asked him any questions after the bar.

But that had been enough. He'd proudly told his captors that his angel would come. Why shouldn't he? God brought Matthew into his life. God would bring him back. His angel would save him, maybe rebuild the little church orphanage and find a new priest to watch the children of the street.

He'd experienced dangers of which adults of most of the world would never imagine. And yet, he held the faith of a saint.

He knocked on the door again. "I need to go to the bathroom."

Clomping in the hallway. Pindip moved back from the door. It opened slowly, cautiously.

"Come with me," said the skinny onion man. He was eating some kind of sandwich, something the foreigners had brought with them.

The man moved aside to let him pass. The boy strolled past, already knowing the way. Three steps out, he saw the man take another bite of his meal. That's when he made his move. He stomped as hard as he could, scraping the side of his well-worn shoe down the man's shin.

He didn't wait to see what happened next. He ran, as fast as he could, as fast as his little conditioned legs would take him.

He made it to the stairs. No one there. He bounded down as a roar came from behind. Skinny onion man had collected himself.

He tried to figure the way out. He'd been blindfolded coming in. But this was someone's house, he knew that now. How different could the layout be from any other?

An empty room greeted him at the bottom of the stairs, the man close behind. Still Pindip did not panic. He'd been chased before. Many times. Sometimes daily. It was his life. Always the quarry never the hunter.

He slipped past a discarded sofa and toward what he assumed was the back of the house. He hadn't seen a single door yet, nor a window to get his bearings.

He made another turn, thinking this was it, knowing that he was close.

He crashed into the powerful form of the massive Russian. He bounced off only to be scooped up by the front of his shirt. He squirmed, tried to get away. There was the door. He saw sunlight. So close.

The Russian squeezed, not enough to choke the boy, just to get his attention. And get his attention it did.

Their eyes met, Pindip trying his best to show that he was unafraid.

My angel is coming, he thought silently.

"Where are you going, little rat?"

Unlike the skinny onion man, this man's breath smelled of toothpaste. The contradiction of his intimidating form and minty fresh breath stunned Pindip. He didn't know why. Maybe it was because he'd assumed bad men had bad smells.

"I... "

The skinny man came into the room.

"It's your job to watch him," the larger Russian said.

"He's fast."

The leader didn't look upset. Pindip would've expected a slap or maybe just getting thrown against a wall. Neither option materialized. Instead, the musclebound hulk set Pindip down on the ground.

"Get him some food."

He turned and went about his morning.

"He's coming," Pindip said, puffing out his chest to show he was unafraid of this man and his compatriots.

The Russian looked back. His placid face turned into a thin smile that turned into something else. Not a snarl. Not a grimace. Something base and... evil.

"I look forward to meeting your angel, Pindip. We have so much to talk about."

And with that, the man strode away. And the skinny onion man yanked Pindip off his feet and dragged him to the bathroom.

CHAPTER TWENTY-EIGHT

Morning came, and a taxi honked from the street outside the house.

"Time to roll," Wilcox announced, snatching the last piece of bacon from his plate and downing the remnants of his coffee.

Cal grabbed his backpack, Liberty stretching at his side.

"Where to?"

"That's a surprise."

"Of course it is."

"You know there's a part of you that wouldn't want me to give away the surprise."

Wilcox's eyes were twinkling. Really twinkling.

They piled in the taxi. When the driver balked at having a dog in the car, Wilcox gave him a twenty and told him to drive to the airport, now.

Pictures of ordinary life flew by on the short trip to their next hop. Cal watched them flow by, soaking them up and imprinting them with his own snapshot memories. He caught glimpses of old friends gathered on sidewalks, cigarettes dangling from smiling lips. His mother and father, holding hands as they walked into a Subway sandwich shop in a shopping center with half the store front empty. His dead fiancée, Jessica, sitting on a bench waiting for a bus.

Why the dead? Was this a portent of things to come? Was he having illusions of the future, or were the dead welcoming him to their world, the two universes merging?

"Hey, we're here."

Cal looked up. Wilcox was out of the cab, bag strapped, Liberty waiting by his side. He hadn't even registered arriving. Strange. Like he had one foot here and one foot...

No use thinking on that now.

Another private jet revved its engines.

"Come on," Wilcox said, pulling a treat from his pocket and giving it to Liberty, who snatched it up like it'd been offered by Cal himself. Terrific. No more wariness of the criminal within. It was as if Wilcox's chameleon status was recognized across species. The two had become friends, and after the first treat she sat down expectantly.

"Sorry," Cal said, scooting off the seat.

"All here then?"

Reading his mind again, the bastard.

"Completely."

They boarded the plane, the crew deferential. Wilcox was polite, even benevolent. He had them eating out of his hand before takeoff.

It made Cal wonder. It made him think. It made him shift.

CHAPTER TWENTY-NINE

Matthew Wilcox.

So much wrapped into a first and last name.

Matthew Wilcox.

A walking contradiction.

I'd come into this thinking one thing, believing that the answer to the riddle was a bullet through the man's forehead. That worked for most men. No offense to the ladies, unless that's something you had in mind.

Matthew Wilcox.

Assassin.

Assassin. Why do we immediately put a label on things we think we understand? A killer is not always an assassin but an assassin is always a killer. I am a killer. Daniel Briggs is a killer. Master Sergeant Willie Trent is a killer. We're killers because we've killed people. Bad people for sure, but still killed, dead, buried, gone.

Does that make us bad people? Murderers? I don't think so. I think I can say with 99.99% accuracy that Briggs doesn't look at us that way. But what would others think?

The average American, hell the average world citizen might look at us the way I've looked at Wilcox.

Matthew Wilcox.

Hero?

No. That's going too far.

Or is it?

He hasn't shown me an evil side. He saved some kids. He's done the right thing. Hell, Liberty likes him. My dad always said that dogs can see the soul of a man. That's one of their gifts. They sniff out evil like saints sniff out pain.

Dad. I wish he was here. He'd tell me what to do. He'd help me dissect it all. He'd know exactly what I was supposed to do.

Dad.

Liar?

Cheat?

Father.

The hate and anger from the mountain fades. I see now that the circumstance in which I found myself exacerbated my basest thoughts. Like a stray dog chained to a stake, I retreated to caveman status, grumbling and barely intelligible.

Dad.

Where are you?

Are you watching me?

What should I do?

I've never had a problem with indecision. Have I said that before? Give me a choice between A and B and BAM I'm making the call. Either that or I'm making up an Option C.

It's the Marine in me. It's my dad in me.

Dad.

Why did you do it?

A moment of weakness? A weeklong tryst? An argument with mom?

Sons are supposed to forgive their fathers, aren't they?

This feels so stupid, so juvenile. I'd know them in the end. My dad's alleged indiscretions were years before. Obviously, my parents had gotten past it. Hadn't they?

Had my father told my mom about the affair?

Wow.

There it is.

Is that what I've been looking for?

It was sitting right there. Not the act. Not the gory detail. I want to know if my mom knew, how the affair affected her.

Yeah. Here we go now, Cal. Getting to the meat of your insecurity.

Insecurity.

Uh huh. That's it too. Like an alcoholic or doper passing his recessive genes to his son, did my dad pass his proclivities to me? That's why I'd sent Diane away, wasn't it?

Shut up, Cal. Shut up and focus. A billion and half poor bastards have it worse than you. At least you've got friends, a place to sleep, food to eat. Be grateful for the little things. Why can't you be grateful for the little things?

Maybe it's because I see a big thing coming. But what is it, and when will it march over the horizon?

CHAPTER THIRTY

The Philippines was hotter than Cal remembered. He'd only been to Manila once. He didn't really like the place, but the food wasn't half bad. He'd served with plenty of Filipinos in the Corps. But he saw the reason why many had left. The shanty towns rolled by as they cruised on to their next destination.

Wilcox was at the wheel of a ten-year-old Range Rover, aviator sunglasses dulling the sun. Johnny Cash grumbled along with them, almost matching the beat of the potholes they hit along the way.

"Beautiful country," Wilcox said, pointing to a row of new homes along the coast.

"Sure."

Wilcox glanced over. "Hey, what's put the run in your panty-hose, pal?"

"Excuse me?"

"You look like a bulldog chewing a wasp."

"I just want to know what we're doing here."

Wilcox whistled along with Cash for a couples of bars. Liberty's ear perked up at the sound. Her head was resting on the console between Cal and his companion.

"Johnny Cash got it, man. He'd seen the world. Good and bad. Wish I could've met him. Hey, you're from Nashville. Did you ever get to meet the Cash family?"

Why this? Why now?

"Not me. My dad."

Why did it still feel like he was choking out a chicken bone every time he said the word 'dad'?

"Really? Did he know Johnny?"

"He did."

"Holy crap! Tell me about it. What was he like?"

"I told you, I didn't know him."

"Not your dad. I mean Johnny."

Cal ignored the jibe. He wasn't about to give Wilcox the satisfaction. "Yep. No idea."

"Come on, Cal. Your dad had to tell you something."

"Never did."

Wilcox focused on the road again. "You know, the pissed off routine is getting old."

"What is this, a domestic quarrel?"

"I just thought it'd be nice if you loosened up a bit. Might make for a better all-around performance."

"Sorry, Matthew. Or should I call you *Master* Wilcox? Sorry, Master Wilcox, but the asshole driving this beat up Range Rover is holding me hostage."

"You need to lighten up."

"And you need to tell me what the hell we're doing in the Philippines. Let me guess, you want me to kill the president, start a civil war."

Wilcox's knuckles went white on the steering wheel. The Range Rover swerved. Cal hadn't been watching the road.

They pulled to the side of the busy thoroughfare, Wilcox seething.

I finally got to him, Cal thought.

The man at the wheel reached under the seat and pulled out a handgun, worn but glistening with just enough lubricant on the barrel.

"Take it," Wilcox said, offering it to Cal.

"What for? Russian roulette?"

"I said take it."

Cal hesitated.

"See. You can't even make that call. I'm telling you to take the gun. Take it, you sonofabitch. Shoot me. At least you can try."

They sat there, traffic streaming by, the tension rising in the car. Liberty had scooted to the back seat, panting.

"Take it, pussy."

Cal didn't move. Why?

Wilcox shook his head, slapped the steering wheel with his open palm. "I've given you enough time. You decide or you die. I don't have time, the *world* doesn't have time for your indecision."

The pistol went back to its hiding space under the seat and Wilcox revved the engine, shooting back onto the road as the rear of vehicle fishtailed.

Neither man spoke for a good five minutes. Cal was trying to figure out what had just happened. Wilcox had given him the opening. He'd even offered the weapon. And Cal hadn't taken it. What the hell was wrong with him?

The Range Rover took a hairpin right turn and came to skidding halt. Cal's eyes whipped to Wilcox, but his companion was looking straight through the windshield. Cal's eyes went that way, saw the small chapel that could've been white once, a brilliant speck in the lush green landscape of the Philippine island. But now it was gray in the places Cal could actually see it. The rest was engulfed in black, and angry flames, and sending tendrils up the cross at the highest gable. When the cross fell forward, Wilcox rushed from the car.

CHAPTER THIRTY-ONE

C al just sat there, watching. He had every advantage now. The Range Rover. The gun. All their belongings. Sure, he still had the electric watch strapped to his wrist, but...

Liberty made the choice for him, bolting from the driver's side door, following her new friend.

"Dammit."

Cal opened his door, meaning to rush out and retrieve the dog. Wilcox was almost upon the flames now, yelling something.

Cal found his legs moving, soon running.

"Pindip!" Wilcox shouted, still controlled. "Father Francis!"

No one appeared to answer his calls.

Part of the roof caved in, sending burning embers too close for comfort. Wilcox barely registered the danger. He was skirting the building now, eyes wide.

Just then a form darted from the tree line. Cal saw it first and then Liberty. Her teeth bared for the slightest moment. Until she saw what Cal saw: It was a boy. He ran, his tiny legs propelling him toward Wilcox.

"Matthew!" the boy screamed.

Wilcox turned. He was on the wrong side of the building,

couldn't see the boy. He ran toward the sound of the child who called over and over again.

They saw each other and Wilcox closed the gap, scooping the boy up in his arms.

What the...?

Surprises galore.

But while man and boy sunk to the ground hugging, another surprise reared its ugly head. A group of men, one massive and leading the way, came out of the tree line, right where the kid had appeared.

Cal whistled, getting Wilcox's attention, pointing to the tree line. Wilcox whispered something to the boy. There was hesitation there, then the boy ran towards Cal. Wilcox marched straight at the men, five in all strolling towards the burning chapel.

The boy made it to Cal. "Come. The angel says we should get in the car."

The angel?

Wilcox wasn't armed. Or was he?

Twenty feet before the group reached their target. Cal figured he had just enough time to reach the Range Rover, get the pistol under the front seat and come to Wilcox's aid.

But why? He didn't even know who the strangers were. For all he knew they could be authorities, maybe Americans.

No. That was wrong. The way they carried themselves. The hard faces that bore the stamp of wars that went back hundreds of years. There's a look to the type of thug that is reared in such a land.

Cal scooped the boy up. Liberty was barking now, following Cal. But her head jerked frantically back and forth between him and the coming confrontation. Two of the men broke off and hurried towards Cal.

His legs were moving now. The child weighed nothing and smelled of sweat and day-old food, like he hadn't bathed in weeks.

Cal made it to the car, deposited the boy in the passenger seat, then retrieved the gun. Liberty was going crazy now, tail straight, snarling and barking like nothing Cal had ever seen.

Wilcox had made it to within five feet of the remaining three. Now the two breakoffs were jogging closer to the Range Rover.

"Go!" Wilcox called out, momentarily looking at Cal. There was a determined resignation there. He saw Wilcox reach down to his belt. The group stiffened, hands shifting oversized shirts, ready to pull their weapon. They looked more curious than concerned. Maybe it was their numbers.

The electric leash on his wrist clicked. The wristwatch's clasp was undone, the power gone. All he had to do was wriggle his wrist for the thing to fall off. It slipped to the floorboard.

He didn't hesitate. "Liberty! Come!"

The dog took one last look Wilcox's way, then scrambled in over Cal and into the back seat. The stalkers were ten feet from the SUV when Cal gunned the sturdy engine and they were off. A flare of dirt sprayed behind him, and the last thing Cal saw of the confrontation was three men falling over Wilcox, fists flying.

CHAPTER THIRTY-TWO

In and out of traffic they weaved. The boy was crying, calling out, "Matthew, Matthew!"

"It's gonna be okay, kid."

He tried to comfort the boy to no avail. Liberty sniffed and nudged the boy, letting out a few squeaking whines of her own.

"Matthew! Matthew!"

When they were a safe enough distance away, they pulled off the busy thoroughfare. He felt the warm breeze on his wrist. He was free. Wilcox was either beat to a pulp or in custody or dead. Why didn't any of these options bother Cal now? A few minutes before... no that wasn't right. A few minutes before he'd refused the pistol that could've ended it all.

Pindip didn't know the man driving. He didn't care. He only cared about one thing. They'd left his angel behind.

Pindip saw the fists fly. He knew what that meant. No fear from his angel as he waded into the Russians, like a man resigned to his fate. It made Pindip think of an old man he'd seen once, hunched to the point where his torso almost touched his legs. Poor man. He had walked past Pindip, who'd been sitting on the side of the train tracks waiting for the next train to come. He liked watching, imagining that one day he would jump on a train, maybe when he was older, strong enough to make the leap. Not that day and not for many more.

That day the old man had stepped to the track, tapped it with his gnarled walking stick, then put his foot on the rail.

"It's coming," the man said conversationally.

"Yes."

"You should move back."

"Why? I always sit here."

"You should move back."

Though he was not accustomed to taking orders from broken old men, something in the man's tone made him move, and he did so while still watching the man. The ancient hunchback tried to raise his face to the sky but his back wouldn't allow it. Pindip thought he saw a single tear drop from the old man's hollow eyes.

The train whistle blew. Pindip picked up a rock. He liked to try to hit the track right before the train hit one exact spot. A race to the divot on the rail.

The rock nestled into Pindip's hand as he watched the old man, still standing one step from the track.

What is he doing? Pindip thought. Waiting for someone on the train?

But that didn't make sense. The station was half a mile away. If the old man...

Then it had clicked. In the Philippines, both the very young and the very old share an equal awareness of the fragility of life.

"Hey," Pindip said as the train came into view.

The old man didn't look back. "Stay back, boy."

The whistle blew. "You should move."

"Stay back."

Pindip's heart sped up a click and a half. He jumped to his feet.

The train whistle blew again.

The old man turned, looked right at Pindip. In that moment the boy saw the eyes, glistening, unafraid. Time slowed. The man's arms went out wide. The train whistle blared, a stabbing pain in his ears.

He saw the old man's lips move.

Pindip screamed, a string of anguished gibberish, as the old man fell back, his final act timed perfectly.

Gone, like he'd never been. Swept away with the angry roar of the train.

THAT'S how Pindip felt when he'd seen Matthew make his move.

"Matthew! Matthew!" he screamed, again and again until his throat shredded itself.

THE KID WOULDN'T STOP. What was his connection to Wilcox? It couldn't be his son.

"Hey, come on, buddy. He'll be okay."

It was far from the truth, but something about the words gave the boy pause. The screams stopped. Hope laced in tears.

"What's your name?"

"Pindip," the boy sniffled.

"Pindip. Cool name. Hey, can you tell me where you live, Pindip? Where are your parents?"

Cal knew the answer before it came from the boy's lips.

"Dead."

No emotion there. Just the statement of fact. A past misery relegated to the shelves of eternity.

"Why don't I take you home?"

"No home."

"Was that your home, the church?"

Pindip nodded. His lower lip trembled, and he said, "Matthew." The name came out pitifully now, like he'd finally figured it all out.

"He'll be okay, I promise."

Why did he say that? He needed to get the hell out of there.

With a quick second thought, he pulled the cell phone from the glove compartment. The same one Wilcox had stashed right after picking up the Range Rover.

"I'm going to call some friends, okay, Pindip? We're going to help Matthew."

Hope returned to the boy's eyes.

Cal turned the phone over in his hand.

Why the hell am I doing this?

CHAPTER THIRTY-THREE

Neil Patel put his fourth Diet Red Bull of the day into the trashcan next to his disheveled desk. He'd spent another long day searching for Cal. Like Wilcox, he'd just disappeared. Nothing on the grid. Every tech skill Neil had compiled over the years had come up with squat.

"Dammit."

His foot tapped absentmindedly. He was the last one left in the War Room, the heart of The Jefferson Group. The others were off getting dinner, taking a rare break from their search.

Two weeks Cal had been gone. Too long. Too many things could've happened.

It was their rock, Daniel Briggs, who'd kept them moving. Just like they'd done when Cal had been captured months earlier, when there was no doubt in Daniel's determination, just a warrior pushing straight on.

I wish I had his confidence, Neil thought, not for the first time.

He turned off the monitor, although his varied programs would continue to scan the world for clues of Cal's whereabouts.

"Time to get some shut eye," Neil said to the empty room. He was hungry but knew he needed to sleep. His night shift would start in a matter of hours. Best to have some sleep in the bag beforehand.

He was just reaching for the handle of the armor-plated door when the phone in the middle of the room rang. Neil froze. There were two land lines coming into TJG headquarters, one was from the president, the other, the emergency line. This was the one ringing. Every TJG operative had the number and the detailed codes to get through.

Neil lunged for the phone, somehow out of breath when he answered.

"PATEL."

Cal couldn't help but smile at the sound of his old friend's voice.

"Neil, it's me."

A long intake of breath.

"Cal, thank God. Where are you? Are you okay? I can get the others. We've been—"

"Neil, I need you to listen to me."

"Sure. Yeah. Just tell me—"

"Listen. I'm somewhere in the Philippines. I need you to shift whatever assets we have. Pull favors if you have to. Move mountains, I don't care what you do, just don't call Brandon."

"Okay."

He heard the questioning in Neil's voice.

"I've got a phone, but I'm sure it's encrypted and impossible to track."

"Can you find another phone?" Neil asked.

"Another phone?"

"Like at a store. Make one call with a temp phone and I can have a GPS lock in minutes."

"I suppose I could."

"Okay. One problem fixed. Next, I need you to go back through flight manifests, ship's crew. I'm looking for a group of five guys. Maybe CCTV picked them up in Manila, some airport. The leader is a big guy. Maybe Russian."

"Yes, they are Russian," Pindip said next to him.

Cal looked at the boy with surprise. "Thanks, kid." He patted Pindip on the shoulder.

"Who was that?" Neil asked.

"A friend. So yeah, they're Russians." Cal gave Neil a quick description of the one's he'd seen. It wasn't perfect, but it was something.

"Okay. I'll see what I can do." A pause on Neil's end. "Just a heads up, Cal, this might take a while."

"That's okay. Just start looking."

"We will. Hey, Cal, I was wondering, I mean we were wondering if—"

"I'm fine."

"Well, thank God for that. But what I was asking—"

"Neil, listen. I know what you're asking. And I'm much better, actually."

"Really?"

"Yeah, really. I'm good, I promise."

"That's great." Neil sounded invigorated now, the uncomfortable voice gone. "Okay, I'll get to work. I assume we'll see you soon?"

"Sure. Yeah. Tell the boys I'll see them soon."

But even as he said it, Cal didn't know if he'd just told another lie.

CHAPTER THIRTY-FOUR

W hy?
     Why did I stay?
What was I expecting?
Between this kid, Pindip, and Matthew...
I don't know what I was thinking.

Maybe that was it. I was done thinking. The thaw on my soul had taken hold, the numbness gone now. I needed to do something. I wanted to do something.

More than that, I wanted to know the rest of Wilcox's answers.

Just now I remembered a poem that one of my English teachers at UVA had us read. In it, the guy described the feeling of sitting in a bathtub as the water lets out. Feeling the body grow heavier as you leave the realm of comfort, of relaxation. Of delusion.

Wonder what made me think of that.

CHAPTER THIRTY-FIVE

CHARLOTTESVILLE, VIRGINIA

"Tell me exactly what he said," Daniel Briggs said to Neil as they hurried to pack their mission gear.

Neil told him.

"How did he sound?"

"It's recorded if you want to hear."

"No, just tell me."

"He sounded, well, good. Better."

"You're sure."

"Yeah."

Daniel checked his weapon load, extra ammunition, emergency rations, just in case.

"Top, how long until the brothers have the plane at the airport?"

"Ray says thirty minutes. J.P. says twenty-five. I'm going with Ray for safety."

"Wait," said Neil. "Ray and J.P. are brothers?"

Daniel looked sideways at the man. "You didn't know that?"

"Five years as our resident pilots and I had no idea."

Daniel gave him a wary look.

Neil shrugged. "I thought they just liked each other's company."

Daniel shook it off. "Let's hit the road."

MSgt Trent hefted his pack onto his shoulder. "So, we got you, Neil, Gaucho, and myself. You sure we don't need more men?"

"I'm sure. We don't know what we're getting into. Best to leave the rest behind."

"How about we take—"

"No, Top. This is it."

Top knew better than to argue with Daniel. When Cal was away, Daniel was in charge. Even if that weren't the case, not a person at TJG could remember a time that Daniel's advice hadn't been taken as gospel.

"Very well, Marine," Top said, headed to the front door. "Off we go."

CHAPTER THIRTY-SIX

The kid was ravenous. Cal had stopped at a roadside food stand. Pindip had ordered for them both, no hesitation.

"Slow down, buddy, you don't want to choke."

Cal wasn't hungry but who knew when he'd eat again. It helped that the cart's mystery meat was as good as it smelled.

"Storm coming," Pindip said around a mouthful.

Cal looked up at the sky. They'd made an impromptu picnic on the tailgate of the Range Rover. Not a cloud in the sky.

"Looks clear to me."

"Storm coming," the kid repeated, wolfing down the rest of the meal. Cal handed him the rest of his, which the boy grabbed eagerly.

What Cal really wanted to do was quiz the kid some more. Up until now Pindip had played it safe, as if preserving whatever relationship he had with Wilcox.

"So, the Russians..."

"Bad guys."

"Yeah. I picked up on that." Cal searched for the right questions. While Pindip was a wily six-year-old, conversation was still limited. Pindip's English seemed to revolve around popular Americanisms rather than a real grasp of the language.

"Where did they keep you?"

Pindip shook his head. "Beats me."

"Did they hurt you?"

Pindip nodded. "Hit me. Kick once."

The answer made Cal's stomach turn.

"Okay, do you remember how long they drove to where you saw Matthew?"

Pindip's face registered confusion. He didn't understand.

Cal pointed to his watch. "Time. How much time from house to Matthew?"

Another shake of the little head.

This was going nowhere. While Cal searched for the right question, Pindip finished the rest of Cal's meal, letting out a muted burp. Liberty had taken to the boy immediately, nestling next to him on the tailgate.

"Good boy, doggie," Pindip said, stroking Liberty's coat. She snuggled closer, almost on his lap now. "When we find Matthew?"

The meal seemed to calm Pindip's previous hysteria. Cal had really thought the kid was going crazy.

"We're gonna find him, kid. We just need to figure out how. Hey, do you know where I can buy a phone?"

Pindip pointing to the phone on Cal's lap.

"No, I need a new phone. Where can I buy one?"

The boy thought about it for a moment and then said, "Town," and pointed the way they'd been going.

"They have a store?"

"Yes."

"Good let's start there, and then we can find out how to find Matthew."

The boy sprang from his seated position and hurried to the front passenger seat.

. . .

TWO HOURS and much haggling later, Cal had a new phone. It was a throwback, a flip model that took forever to get a signal. Once he had one, he was able to make a call to Neil who was now in the air with the rest of the TJG team.

"I've got your location. Make sure you leave the phone on," Neil instructed. "Hey, Daniel wants to talk to you."

"Okay," Cal said, unsure of whether he was ready to speak to the sniper.

"Cal." The reassuring voice.

"Hey"

"What's the situation?"

"I can't... a little early to tell."

"I mean with you."

Cal grimaced inwardly. He wasn't ready to talk about his feelings, let alone the situation with Wilcox since he didn't know for sure himself.

"I'm good."

"Yeah?"

"Yeah. Now can we get down to business?"

"I thought we were."

Cal couldn't help but smile. "Of course we are. Hey, it's good to hear your voice."

"Ditto. We'll see you soon, Cal. Don't skip ahead."

"I won't."

Another lie. He'd already made the decision to go in alone were he to locate Wilcox's whereabouts. Time was short and he was ready.

"Forgot to ask Neil, what's the forecast for the next two days here?"

"Big storm rolling in. We may have bumpy ride in."

So the kid had been right. Cal gave Pindip a reassuring wink.

"You guys be careful," he said. "I'll be waiting."

No reply came. He looked down at the phone and saw that he'd lost the signal. He wondered if that meant that Neil couldn't track him.

Did it really matter?

They would either be in time to help or in time to collect his body.

CHAPTER THIRTY-SEVEN

The right came slow, too slow, crashing into Wilcox's rib cage. He tried to go with it, absorb some of the spent energy.

No good. The hit still felt like a stab in the ribs.

He grunted without wanting to. At this, the large Russian grinned.

"Fun, no?" the big man asked.

"Yeah. Fun. Like cancer."

This had started when the Russian had told Wilcox that his name was Boris. Wilcox had laughed obnoxiously at it, even going so far as to do an impression for the man, saying something about Moose and Squirrel. Then came the right to the ribs.

Now Boris grinned, swinging again, sending more searing pain through Wilcox's body.

He was strung up in a wood hut. A wood fucking hut. Like something out of a Rambo movie.

"Hey, you mind if we take a break? I need to take a leak."

Boris's smile waned.

"You even know what 'leak' means, you simian?"

The confused look. Boris tried to grin through the confusion.

Just to make sure that the idiot knew he was being made fun of, Wilcox flashed him a mocking grin.

"Yeah, you, the knuckle-dragger with the face like a zookeeper's nightmare."

The Russian's grin disappeared. There was nervous chuckling from the peanut gallery – miniature versions of their leader, the same hard look of men who'd spent their adult lives doing dirty deeds. Tattoos were barely visible under short sleeves that looked like prison tats.

"Hey," said Wilcox, looking over at them, "just curious. Which one of you takes it up the ass from Boris here?"

This they all understood. No chuckles this time.

"I guess you all take turns in the barrel, huh?"

"You funny guy," Boris said, massaging his knuckles. They were as rough as a rind of cheese. He'd put his fists to good use over the years.

"Yeah," said Wilcox, "I'm a funny guy who doesn't give a shit about you and your women back there."

Grumbling from the peanut gallery. Snippets of Russian. They were begging their leader to pound the impudent American.

Go for it, Boris, Wilcox thought.

He knew pain. He'd lived pain. Physical pain was temporary when no emotion was involved. His body was the physical manifestation of what he'd become. The rest of the world could regret their missed opportunities. The thirty-year-old father who regretted not spending more time with his children. The fortysomething woman who wished she'd driven to LA to become an actress. The eighty-year-old veteran whose dying thought looped around his regret for not spending more time with his war buddies.

Not Wilcox. Never Wilcox.

He'd lived the pain and come out stronger. And now, with Cal safe, his life's work was complete.

Almost.

If he was being completely honest, he did have one regret. One thing that he'd wanted to see. He wanted to see Cal come to his full potential. Wilcox wanted to see the avenging angel that Cal could – no, *would* become. As good as Matthew. Better even.

That thought made him grin. He spit a wad of bloody phlegm onto the wood floor.

"Okay, you simpering primate, what's next? I'm getting bored."

The next fist smashed him to blackness.

CHAPTER THIRTY-EIGHT

Was this another angel?

This man was like Matthew. Kind. Different than the men he'd grown up with in the village. There was no conniving in his manner. He was a man to look up to.

"Okay, buddy. I've got some friends coming soon. Do you know of a good place where we can wait for them?"

A gust of wind teetered the trees outside the Range Rover.

"Storm."

"Yeah, you were right. So do you know where we can wait?"

"Hotel not far."

"I don't have any more money," Cal said. The American had searched every inch of the vehicle. All he'd been able to find was the small stash he'd used to buy their meal.

Pindip mulled their predicament for a minute. He knew of many places to hide, but most were too small for the American. Besides, Pindip wanted somewhere safe, warm. They needed shelter from the coming storm.

"Yes. I know place."

The American grinned and started the engine. It came to life then died with a cough.

Matthew's friend made a face and looked at the dash.

THEY MADE their way into another hamlet. There were the usual stares from the locals. Pindip saw them. They saw him. He knew they wondered. A white man with a Filipino boy in the car. He wanted to tell them that this wasn't what they thought.

This man was another angel.

"We find Matthew?"

"Yeah. We're gonna find him, kid."

Just then, Pindip had an idea. "Turn here."

The Range Rover skidded into the right turn, narrowly missing a waddling pedestrian.

Cal grimaced. "How 'bout a little notice next time, okay?"

It wasn't a scolding, and Pindip knew it. There'd been plenty of scoldings during his time on the street.

"Sorry," Pindip said. "Up there. Turn."

There was only one way to go now. The instructions were unnecessary, but Pindip didn't want to disappoint the man named Cal. A good man. Another angel.

They made the turn. A sheet of rain made Cal switch on the wiper blades. The Range Rover slowed and Pindip leaned forward to see better.

"There." Pindip pointed. There was a structure up ahead. A place Pindip never dared visit before. But he had a feeling that this man Cal could handle it. If Matthew could, then this new angel could.

The Range Rover slid into a spot next to a hulk of some long lost rusty heap.

"What is this place?" Cal asked.

"Man inside. He know where to find Matthew."

"You sure?"

But Pindip wasn't entirely sure. He had to try. No not he. *They* had to try. He wasn't alone this time and Pindip meant to keep it that way.

"Yes. We find where Matthew is."

CHAPTER THIRTY-NINE

Cal smelled the place as soon as he stepped from the Range Rover. It gagged him. Pindip didn't seem to mind it. What was it? Burning rotted flesh?

Pindip rushed to the tiny awning out of the rain and waited.

Cal exhaled and ran to join him, soaked to his underwear by the time he got there. The storm was picking up. He wondered if their ride would be there when he emerged.

Pindip knocked hesitantly on the door.

There was a croak of a sound from inside.

Pindip took that as the cue to open the door. When the door creaked on its hinges, the smell almost overpowered Cal this time. The boy went straight in, already jabbering in his native tongue. He even bowed.

Cal didn't want to close the door, but he did. He bit back the bile rising from the pit of his stomach.

The place was dark, the gloom almost as overpowering as the stench. Then he saw it, the fire, a pit of glowing coals in the center of the main room. There was a circular wall of stone, like a campfire built inside. Cal saw the man beyond the fire, a disproportioned figure he couldn't quite make out. The croaking man addressed Pindip in lilting tongue. He sounded like what Cal thought would happen if a dying alcoholic and a chronic smoker mated and spewed forth a twisted old man.

There was something next to the fire. The source of the smell? A metal tray, smoke rising from the mound of whatever substance it was. The old man picked a piece with his fingers. Cal heard the sizzle as juice hit the metal.

The piece went into the man's mouth, the sight taking Cal's stomach into a new round of churning.

Pindip's animation increased, gesturing with his hands like he was painting a portrait on an invisible wall. That went on for a few minutes, the man picking at his food and conversing with the boy.

Then they both turned to him. Cal could see the man's eyes now, not the eyes of an old man, but the eyes of a someone much younger. The body was ancient, the soul still young, probing, searching. He pointed at Cal and said the longest stream of words he'd yet used.

"He wants to know," said Pindip.

"Know what?" Cal asked, his stomach going queasy.

"He..." Pindip searched for the right words. "He says you... interesting."

The boy smiled at finding the correct word.

"What does he want? Money?"

The man shook his head without need for translation.

"He has the bones," said Pindip.

"Bones?"

"For future."

Cal put the pieces together.

"He wants to tell my future?"

Pindip's head bobbed up and down happily.

"Why does he want to tell my future, Pindip?"

The boy asked the man, who responded curtly.

"He... curious."

"Fine. But tell him we don't have much time."

"He knows."

Cal moved forward just as a wave of smoke wafted his way.

He tried to exhale away the gagging smell, but it was no use. The putrescence assaulted him, seemed to seep into his very being. It took every square inch of resolve Cal had to ignore it and move in close to the man. A cragged hand shot out, quick as a jackrabbit.

Cal moved back but the man motioned for his hand. Reluctantly, Cal proffered his hand, cringing as it touched with the grease slicked hand of the other.

The man moved close, holding Cal's hand to the light, turning it this way and that, examining it in the dim firelight. He pointed, tapped out a beat, and nodded, murmuring to himself.

"He says you good man," Pindip translated.

"Great. Can we go now?"

"Not done." The two words came from the man, not Pindip.

The bastard knew English. Of course he did.

A long, brittle nail traced a line down the middle of Cal's palm then went down each digit.

"Good man," the guy confirmed, letting Cal's hand go.

Cal somehow avoided the extreme urge to wipe his hand on his pant leg.

The man shifted again, this time produced a plastic baggie, a Ziploc castoff from the 1980's from the looks of it. As the grinning man held up the clear bag and jiggled it, Cal noticed the black teeth that perfectly mirrored his dark mood.

With a flourish, the man ripped the bag open and cast the bones on the floor. Chicken bones, or maybe human fingers, scattered in a twelve-inch diameter. The man went to his knees like a child looking for worms in the rain. Head bobbing, he touched each and every bone, careful not to disturb whatever otherworldly artist had put them in their exact positions.

One minute. Two minutes. Three. When what Cal estimated was five minutes had gone by, the man rose. He moved so close to Cal that the smell of the man overpowered the rest. Then he spoke, touching Cal on the chest, gently, reverently.

"You find power."

"Power?"

The man nodded gravely. "Power."

"Okay."

The man shook his head, annoyed that Cal didn't understand.

"*Power*." He drew the word out as if doing so would explain the gravity to American standing before him.

Cal mimicked the man's tone. "*Power*."

The man smiled now, the black teeth of a pit fiend.

"Use... careful."

Then the man turned, going back to his original perch.

"That's it?"

Pindip looked from Cal to the man.

"He promise to tell us."

"We're losing time, Pindip. We need to know—"

A flurry of words escaped the man's mouth, setting Pindip back a step. Cal couldn't tell if it was the bad light or not, but it looked like Pindip's face went pale.

"He tell me where."

"Where Matthew is?"

Pindip nodded.

"Where is he?"

The boy didn't answer, just stood rooted to the spot, unmoving.

"Pindip, where do we need to go?"

The boy's eyes swiveled around the room, landing on the man who nodded slowly. Then Pindip's gaze shifted to Cal.

"This place, not good."

The boy seemed to struggle with something.

"The place we go, where Russians took Matthew. Bad. Very bad."

"We have to go then."

Pindip nodded absentmindedly as if in a trance. Cal almost had to drag him out of the reeking building.

Cal heard one last thing as they pushed through the door and out into the fresh air of pouring rain. The fortune teller laughed, a rude cackle of anticipation, a mocking laugh that followed the traveling companions back to their ride.

CHAPTER FORTY

Back and forth.
Back and forth.

Flitting images. Blurs of color. Not really colors, more like blurs of black and lighter black. What was that color? Oh yeah, gray. And white. Was white a color? Yeah it was. White was a color, just like black, and gray. But they weren't real colors. Real colors...

Smack.

The pain radiating down his leg jolted Wilcox to finer consciousness.

Smack.

Not excruciating pain. Just enough pain. Like an animal picking him to make sure he was still there.

Smack!

Harder now, more insistent.

Wilcox opened his eyes farther, colors coming now, but they were the just dull browns, the rust of week-old blood on a dress shirt.

His tongue shifted inside his mouth, trying to work. Nope. No saliva.

Water, he tried to say, but realized it was just in his head.

He said it this time. "*Water.*"

The one in his head had been louder.

Something splashed his face.

Water.

His tongue reached out, licked what he could that was dripping down his face.

When he shifted to try and lift his head, his bound arms screamed and so did he, almost.

Wilcox willed his body to wake, took in shallow breaths. That's all his contorted body would allow.

In and out. In and out came the gasps.

"Water," he said again, still unable to see anyone nearby.

Another splash on his face. Another hesitant licking of lips. At least now he could move his tongue. Such a small thing, using one's tongue. And yet, when you can't...

Don't wallow in it, Wilcox told himself. Snap out of it.

Eyes eased open one last time. It took gargantuan effort to do so, like he'd been asleep for ten years.

"Good evening," came the Russian-laced voice.

Wilcox shifting, sending a new round of screams up and down his body.

"Mom?"

The Russian drifted into view, picking up the prisoner's chin.

"Wake up."

"Mom? Is it time for school already?"

Wilcox could hear his own voice, more guttural croak than human.

He got a smack in the face for his efforts.

"Ahh, come on, Mom. I was just finishing this great dream. I was under the bleachers with Susie Wilks." His lips smacked. "Best taste I've had in ages. Must be the lip gloss. I didn't know I could taste lip gloss in a dream. What do you think it means, Mommy?"

Confusion stamped on the Russian's meathead face.

"Mommy? Can I have some breakfast now? Pancakes with chocolate chips. And that thick bacon from the farm. You know the stuff I'm talking about."

Voice clearing now. Mind too.

"Crazy American."

The hacks came from deep within Wilcox, sickly, like the rattle of cancer. Coughs for days.

Boris took pity on Wilcox, grabbing a water bottle from a stack in the corner. At least Wilcox could see that far now. Next to the water was a disheveled stack of beer and other snacks. For the troops. How long had he been out?

The crack of the water bottle's seal was magic to Wilcox's ears. He puckered his lips, at least tried to through the hacks and fits.

Water spilled from the bottle. He lapped eagerly, getting barely more than half a mouthful.

"Closer," he rasped.

Boris complied.

Wilcox saw him move closer. The water bottle touched his lips. Into it now. Sweet delicious nectar of heaven. In a second.

Boris the moron moved in.

Wilcox lunged, his entire body moving like an eel writhing one last time on land before getting the fishmonger's cruel blade.

Only this time, the eel won.

Wilcox's teeth latched onto Boris's pinky finger.

Bon appetite.

The pinky was no match for chomping teeth. Rip, clean through.

Boris roared, blood spewed forth, flooding his mouth, then spurting onto his face and out into the air.

Wilcox crunched down, grinning at the Russian's face through his impromptu meal.

To Boris's credit, he showed very little pain. He ripped a shred from his shirt, wrapped his hand gingerly, and then faced Wilcox.

"Pay time, American."

The bloody digit, now so mutilated that no doctor in their right mind would try to reattach the thing, shifted in Wilcox's mouth. Not so bad really.

He spit the pinky out, garnering at least one shocked gasp from Boris's friends.

"Chew on that, assholes. What about you, nine fingers? Got anything else?"

Boris looked down at the bloody mass that was once his pinky. He bent down, like he'd just seen a swallow fly smack into a window. He even poked it, much like a curious child might.

Eyes came up, then the rest of the hulking man.

The wad of spit came first, hitting Wilcox in the side of the face.

"Now that's just disgusting. Poor taste, Boris." Wilcox moved his jaw around. "Speaking of taste, that pinky could've used a little Tabasco. You know what Tabasco is, you ignorant prick?"

Boring eyes from Boris.

Wilcox saw it coming. The hammer of Boris's fist came crashing. Rather than move out of the way, Wilcox raised his face as much as he could, rising to meet the blow.

And just like he knew it would, the hammer sent him spinning back into the dark unconscious.

CHAPTER FORTY-ONE

Pindip had ridden mostly mute after the visit to the putrid cabin. Cal still felt like he could've bathed for a week and still not gotten the smell cleansed from his body. He didn't ask the boy what the man had been eating. No sense adding to the rumble in his stomach.

To the kid's credit, he gave flawless directions, so accurate that a stranger might've assumed that Pindip had laid the road himself.

"Left here... right up ahead."

Cal kept it slow. The rain sent a steady sheet of water from the clouds. Not that he could see beyond the beams of the Range Rover. The endless buckets of water dumping from above caused a condition known to meteorologists as a *"big fucking mess"*.

Even the pavement they hit was more running river than concrete for the vehicle's tires to hold onto. Thank God Wilcox hadn't left a Kia for them to drive.

"Turn right." Pindip pointed. Cal squinted.

There was a clump of sad trees up ahead – willows with nothing left to weep for.

Cal made the turn slowly, inching along through the torrent of water rushing in the opposite direction. Mud did its best to suck them in halfway into the turn. It took just enough pressure on the gas, just the right turn of the wheel, to get them going along.

"What is this place, Pindip, the place we're going?"

The boy responded as if lost in a dream. "Ghosts."

"Ghosts?"

The boy struggled for the word. "Haunted."

"You sure, buddy? Last time I checked there's no such thing as ghosts. No goblins either."

"Yes, ghosts. Many ghosts."

"Hmm. Too bad we didn't bring the Ghostbusters. You even seen that movie?"

Pindip's face brightened for what seemed like the first time.

"Ghostbusters?"

"Yeah, Ghostbusters. I prefer the original, the one with Bill Murray."

"Stay-Puft Marshmallow Man."

Cal shot the boy a surprised glance.

"Yeah, that thing freaked me out as a kid. How did you watch Ghostbusters?"

Pindip directed his gaze back to front, pointing out a fallen tree up ahead.

"I watch many movie. And Matthew... he... he buy movies for the church."

"You like American movies?"

"Yes. My favorite."

"That's good, really good. Well, you remember how the Ghostbusters kicked those ghosts butts?"

"Yes. *Who you gonna call?*" For the first time, his English was flawless.

That set Cal back. He thought... then he remembered the

scene in the original 80s movie where Sigourney Weaver and Rick Moranis had turned into demons.

"The key master and the gate keeper," Cal recited.

Pindip's head bobbed. "Devil dogs."

"I never thought about it that way. I guess you're right. Devil dogs." Cal tried to think, tried to get past the words. *Devil dogs.* It felt like an omen, but an omen for what? "So, you remember how the Ghostbusters were in a lot of trouble? The devil dogs and that demon lady—"

"And the marshmallow man."

"Yeah, right. And the marshmallow man. Well, you remember how they tried to get the Ghostbusters? Tried to kill them?"

"Yes."

"Right, well, so all this bad stuff happens. The ghostbusters get thrown in jail by the jerk from the EPA, the devil dogs protect the demon. The marshmallow man wants to squash them. And still they come out on top. The good guys win."

Faint understanding on Pindip's face.

"The good guys win," Cal repeated. He didn't have kids. He didn't know how to talk to them.

"Good guys. Matthew is good guy."

That made something in Cal twist like a knot that had been tied the wrong way.

"Sure. We're the good guys. We're gonna win."

Pindip looked down at his lap.

"What's wrong?"

The boy didn't look up when he spoke. "Father Francis was good guy. He no win."

Cal had to scour his brain to figure out who the priest was. It had to be the one from the church.

"What happened to the priest?"

"They kill him."

"Who? The Russians?"

"No. Other. My people."

How do you explain to a kid that the good guys don't always win? That was where Cal had been headed, thought he'd gotten the point across. But the quick mind of a six-year-old derailed those plans.

"Okay. Let's start over. You see... I'm not good at this." Cal motioned between the two of them. "I don't have kids. I don't have nieces or nephews. I'm learning as I go. Can you help me?"

Now Pindip looked up.

"You no have kids?"

"Not a one, buddy."

Pindip seemed to consider that, his face scrunching in that way that seemed to Cal equal parts "I'm solving a theoretical math problem" and "What should I eat for lunch".

"I help."

"And you have. What I need you to do now is trust me."

"Trust?"

Again, the search for the right word, the right description.

"Believe. I need you to believe that I will save Matthew. Do you understand?"

"I understand."

More strength in the boy now.

"Good."

Cal swerved around a pig that was wallowing in the middle of the road. Close one.

"So look, we'll be there soon. I'll leave you somewhere safe." Now the tricky part. He had to prepare the kid. "If I don't come back..."

"You don't come back?"

The desperation again.

"I'm gonna do my best. I promise. Believe. But..." Why was this so hard? With an adult you just explained the situation. Cal had never been one to mince words. Now the words jumbled in his head, a bunch of Scrabble tiles, unreadable. "Okay, I'm not gonna lie to you. This is dangerous. Very dangerous. But you know that, you've lived it, haven't you?" No answer needed. Cal didn't even know if the boy understood. "I'm leaving this phone with you when I leave. I'll set an alarm. If the alarm goes off and I'm not back, I want you to get out of the car and go."

"Where?"

"Somewhere safe. Can you find a safe place?"

Pindip nodded though the look on his face said it all. He didn't want it to happen.

Then an idea came to Cal like a flash of light in the darkness.

"My friends are coming. You'll like them. Daniel especially. He likes kids. Knows kids. And Neil, well, if you like movies, he can find any one you want."

"Any movie?" Pindip's eyes were wide and searching.

"Yeah, any movie." Back to it Cal. You don't have time. "Like I said, my friends will be here soon. I don't have time to wait around. They might be mad at me, but they won't be mad at you. They'll take care of you. How would you like to go with them? Go to America?"

"With Matthew?"

Don't lie to the kid.

"Maybe. What if we meet you there?"

"How get to America?"

"On an airplane."

"Airplane?" Again, the wonder displayed in technicolor.

"Yep. It's a real beauty. You'll love it."

"Your airplane?" There was pure awe in the kid's voice, like Cal was a king or something. He half-expected the kid to bow and kiss his hand. How did kids split grief and hope in the same moment?

"Yeah. It's mine. But that doesn't matter. You tell them every-thing. They'll take care of you okay?"

Pindip settled back into his seat, thinking. A couple minutes of dodging debris and monsoon rivers later and the boy finally spoke.

"Almost there."

And he was right. Not two minutes later they pulled off the road, vegetation swallowing them whole. Nature taking them into her stranglehold.

"Here."

Pindip pointed up ahead. Nothing that Cal could see beyond the dense vegetation.

"You're sure?"

"Yes."

It took a few minutes of maneuvering to find a place that Cal considered sufficiently concealed. No sense leaving the kid out in the open. Some well-placed branches and no one traipsing through the night would see the Range Rover.

Cal grabbed the cell phone he'd purchased. There was a signal.

"Tell me about what I'm looking for again," Cal said to Pindip.

Pindip explained it again, the detail impressive. Cal had to remind himself that this was a six-year-old. When the boy was done with his analysis, Cal tousled his hair.

"Let me make a quick call, tell my friends where we are."

"You go?"

"Yeah."

"To help Matthew?"

Cal expected the kid to press him to go along. Not that that was going to happen. No matter how scrappy the kid was, hunting killers in a haunted wood wasn't a thing you brought a kid along for, no matter how wily.

"Yes. I'm going to help Matthew."

What if he's dead? Cal thought. Can't think that way.

But as he placed the call to his friends, he couldn't help but wonder how much of the rescue mission was for the boy, and how much of it was for him so he could figure out the rest of the damn story.

CHAPTER FORTY-TWO

"It's Cal," Neil said, handing the sat phone to Daniel. The others leaned in.

"Briggs."

"I'm in position," Cal said.

"What position?"

Daniel looked over at Neil who was trying to pinpoint Cal's location from the cell phone signal. Neil shook his head in answer to Daniel's glance. No lock yet.

"I'm not sure how to describe it. You'll see it when you get here. How long until you're on the ground?"

"Ten minutes, fifteen tops."

"How's the flight been?"

"Clean above the clouds. We're just coming down now. Strapped in for the ride."

Cal chuckled on the other end. Daniel strained to hear the subtle inflections in his friend's laugh. No indication of left or right, good or bad.

"How's the kid?"

For some reason, Daniel felt like he had to keep Cal on the

line. It was one of his hunches, something he'd learned to go along with years ago. Let it flow.

"He's good. You'll like him. He's a survivor. Reminds me a little of you.."

"Sounds like you too."

A pause on Cal's end. Daniel thought he'd lost the connection. Maybe it was the turbulence that was shaking the aircraft back and forth.

"You still there?"

Some static and then Cal's voice came back. "I'm still here. Lost you for a second."

"So listen, these Russians, we're pretty sure we got a lead on them."

"Who are they?"

"No one good. Another round of pro-communist thugs making a buck on the free market."

"Who do they work for?"

"That's the thing, we don't know."

"I assume Neil's digging."

"Of course." Keep him on the line. The minutes were ticking down. Daniel figured ten or so minutes until they were on the ground. Then another thirty or more minutes to Cal's location. That wasn't taking in to the account the weather, which tended to play craps with missions like this.

"Hey," said Cal, static perforating his voice, "the kid, I want to make sure he's good after this."

"We can take care of that. Anything in particular?"

Another long pause. Satellites trying to link signals through the mounting storm.

"I thought we could take him back to the States. He doesn't have any family. The kid likes American movies. Can you believe that?"

Where was Cal going? It wasn't like him to wander from the mission talk.

"I don't think that'll be a problem. We'll figure it out."

"Good. I want to make sure he's taken care of."

Pause. Scratching static that made Daniel hold the phone away from his ear. The rest of the team was watching, waiting. They were as worried about Cal as Daniel.

"Briggs, I want you to know... I'm not sure how to say this... you've been a good friend. The best. What you did for me on the mountain, I never got to thank you."

"You'd do the same."

"Sure. But I just wanted to tell you, you know. We don't talk about stuff like that. We just move on, pack our bags and bolt to the next op. I wanted to make sure I told you. Tell the others, will you?"

The gears of worry turned faster and faster in Daniel's head.

"Maybe you should tell them yourself after we're finished."

"Yeah. Yeah, of course. I just... it's been on my mind and I didn't want to forget. You know how I am, always on task."

Pause. Longer string of static and garble.

"Cal?"

"Ye..."

"You still there?"

He looked at Neil who shrugged. Nothing they could do to boost the signal. Neil had already warned them of that fact. If Cal was on a cheap burner phone there was no telling if they'd even get a chance to talk to him.

"I'm... here," Cal's voice finally came through.

"Look, we'll be there in a few minutes. Hang tight. The cavalry's coming."

"Great. Look forward to seeing Gaucho's ugly mug. Tell him he owes me—"

The static now tore apart his words.

"Seriou... friends... lik... ever befo... brothers... eyond... blood..."

The call went out completely as Cal's last word dragged out a full ten seconds, like a digital animation going wonk.

"Lost him," Daniel said, trying to call Cal back. "Nothing, not even a recording."

"We'll see him soon," Top said, downing more water.

"Yeah. We will," Daniel said, although he worried his words may have had less staying power than the last word he'd heard Cal use.

CHAPTER FORTY-THREE

Done, Cal thought. At least the kid would be taken care of. Liberty nudged his arm. He'd almost forgotten she was there.

"Hey, girl." He scratched her behind the ears and she leaned into his caress. His eyes met hers.

He should leave her with the kid. She'd stay. They'd be safe.

But he couldn't. He knew that. Liberty would fight and claw her way out. Cal knew that. They were as linked as good and evil.

"Well, kid, it's time. My friends are on their way."

"I come."

"No. You need to stay here. It's not safe out there."

As if to punctuate that point, lightning struck somewhere close, the resounding thunder shaking the ground all around them. Pindip didn't flinch. Damn tough kid.

"Okay, say goodbye, Liberty."

Pindip reached out and gave the dog a side hug. The dog took it happily, tail wagging.

"Here's the phone. Don't turn it off. That's how my friends will find you, okay?"

Pindip nodded.

"I'll see you soon."

No more time for words. Strapped with Wilcox's gun, Cal gave the boy one more nod and opened the door. The wind howled, trying to tear the door from his grasp.

"Stay here!" he said over the roar, and then slammed the door shut.

The pelting rain soaked him in seconds. He could barely make out Pindip's outline through the downpour. Cal waved, and then he and Liberty took off to find Wilcox.

CHAPTER FORTY-FOUR

When he came to this time, he had the distinct feeling that something had changed. No new smells or sensations. Not even the ache of fresh wounds. Just something, a warrior's sense that the game had changed.

The monsoon still raged overhead, although wherever he was kept was mostly dry. What he would've given for a mouthful of rain, even just enough to swish the blood from his mouth. He could still taste a hint of Russian pinky in there. Not exactly *fois gras*.

The recognition brought on his gag reflex. A long tamped-down memory sparked to life in his brain. Falling off a bike in a resplendent face plant. No one there. Blocks home. A long walk to an empty house. The metaphor of his youth.

Wilcox let the blood seep from his mouth before opening his eyes.

Nothing he did consciously tipped his captors to his lucidity, but they knew anyway. Someone grabbed his chin, forced his face up.

"Wake up, pig."

It was Boris. A good bullet to the forehead would do the roid rager some good.

"Mom, you got real ugly."

The ensuing fist in the gut cut off the smartass in Wilcox. He waited patiently for his breath to return. It seemed to take longer this time. That's when he realized what was different. His head was pounding, not from the blows. He was hanging upside down. The blood and drool were dripping up his forehead, not down.

His breath finally came in a forceful gasp, more show than he liked to give. Another strike against the proprietor.

"Open your eyes."

Wilcox did so, slowly.

Boris was there again, now shirtless. He looked a beefier version of Ivan Drago from Rocky IV.

"Fine. I'm awake. What do you want?"

Had he told them anything in his rising delirium? Probably not. He'd cracked that nut ages ago.

"You talk."

"What do you want to talk about, the weather? Looks pretty crappy to me. Al Roker would probably say that we're in for a real jammer."

The joke went over like kissing a rhino. No effect except for the flair of Boris's nostrils.

"Talk."

"Okay. How about..."

This time Boris head butted him in the sternum. Air whooshed from its proper place in Wilcox's lungs.

But the blow did something else. It knocked him into a swing and made him arch his back, as if the blow was more powerful than it actually was. He'd taken just enough of the impact, knowing it was coming. The arch helped. His core did the rest, going with the moment coming back to his original hanging position.

His timing was perfect. Boris had gotten too close.

Upside down Wilcox whipped his head forward with the swing, his forehead smashing right into Boris's cheekbone. At least the Russian had almost turned.

He staggered back a step, Wilcox grinning despite his breathlessness.

Come on, you sonofabitch, he thought, watching Boris through watery eyes. The goon had a hand on his cheek. At least he was tearing too.

Boris pointed at Wilcox, "Now you feel pain."

"Clever retort," spat Wilcox.

He braced for it. Another punch. A headbutt.

"*Enough*." The even voice cut through Boris's rage, through the sound of the rain hammering overhead. It was spoken in Russian, a language Wilcox spoke fluently.

Wilcox strained through his tears to see who it was. A new player. A voice he didn't recognize from his time in captivity.

Boris took another step forward, hands clenched.

"*I said, enough*."

Boris backed off, his eyes still locked on Wilcox. Whomever the voice belonged to was more than a rung above the musclebound Russian.

"*Leave us*," the voice said. Still no glimpse.

This time Boris didn't hesitate. He left, ushering his pals out first, throwing one final hate dagger at Wilcox. The American puckered his lips and blew him what kiss he could.

The thin door shut. Still no sight of the man with the voice. That voice, clear and silky. Wilcox didn't like it. It was the voice of an authoritarian, a man in charge, a man of confidence. A man like Matthew Wilcox.

"*Who are you?*" the voice said.

He sensed where it came from. A corner of gloom on the far-right side of the room. Definitely not the left, although by the size of the space someone could be hiding there as well. Multiple someones.

"Mickey Mouse. If it's about Minnie's pregnancy, I had nothing to do with it."

Wilcox thought he heard a chuckle. Genuine. Or was that him?

"Please. We know you're American." The voice spoke in English now. Plain, vanilla English. American English. No hint of accent. No way to pinpoint east coast, west coast or somewhere in the middle.

"Who are you?"

"Does it matter?"

"At least let me see you."

"I don't see how that can hurt."

There was a squeaking of a metal chair, probably one of those auditorium cast offs like they have at community centers.

The shadows parted, revealing a man in a rumpled suit. It fit well but was well-soiled by the rain and mud outside. It did little to dampen the man's spirits. He looked like the type who could be plopped down in 150-degree swamp and still sit around looking as placid as a lake in Washington state.

"Boris doesn't like you," the man said, stepping to the middle of the room. He fished something out of his pocket. A packet of Marlboros, the red pack. "Smoke?"

"Why not."

The man tapped a cigarette out of the pack and place it on his lips. He repeated the process, holding the second.

"You promise you won't bite."

"Never on the first date. Besides, something tells me you're not as stupid as Boris."

Another light chuckle, like a polite dinner guest. Both pleasant and accommodating.

The cigarette made its way to Wilcox's lips without incident.

A lighter came next, one of those butane numbers that might take a hurricane head on. There was something on the casing that Wilcox couldn't quite make out. A seal of some kind, like a family crest.

Wilcox sucked in a lungful of smoke, held it, then let it out, the nicotine already smoothing out the kinks.

"Thanks," Wilcox mumbled, careful not to drop the cigarette.

"You're welcome."

The man in the rumpled suit took his time. Wilcox counted five casual inhales and exhales, the smoke hanging in the thick air.

"I have questions," the man said.

"You never told me your name."

"My name doesn't matter."

"Might make the conversation easier."

The man nodded. "You're right. Call me George. And you?"

"I already told you."

"Ah yes, Mickey Mouse. Very well, Mickey. You must give my regards to Goofy when you see him."

The two men shared a smile. Perfect adversaries. Wilcox found that he liked this man.

"So, George, what do I need to do to get out of this place?"

George let out a thin line of smoke that went straight in the air.

"I think you know that won't be the case."

"Oh? Why not?"

"You've done too much."

"I'm not tracking."

"Aren't you?"

Again, the long silence. Wilcox took one last drag and dropped the cigarette to the ground. It hissed when it hit whatever wetness was on the wood floor.

"We've been tracking *you*, Mr. Mouse. I won't bore you with the details. You know where you were. And let me say first, that we got lucky. I applaud you for that fact."

"Thank you very much."

George's eyes went cold. Playtime was over.

"Who are you working for?"

"Walt Disney."

"The CIA? Military? The Chinese?"

"Please. Who would work for the Chinese?"

The cool gaze softened.

"You're right. I apologize. So, which is it? CIA? Freelance?"

Wilcox shifted, the nicotine was going to his head along with all the blood in his body. He shook his head, trying to clear it.

"Any chance you can get me down from here? My head's killing me. I'd like to have a clear head to answer your questions."

George actually considered the question. Wilcox had asked to kill time. For what? He had to win something. As it stood, he was cooked.

George took the long way around the hanging man. Wilcox couldn't see what he was doing, but soon felt himself being lowered to the ground slowly. The top of his head touched the floor, his back next until he was completely on the ground.

"Take a moment. Hanging does a number."

"You got that right."

Wilcox closed his eyes, trying to recalibrate. When he opened again, George was back in his original position.

"Better?"

"Yeah. Thanks."

"What Boris and his friends don't understand is that violence isn't always the way to the truth. Do you agree?"

"To a point. There's something about a dagger to a guy's throat that tends to get answers."

"Would you rather that?"

George reached into his coat and produced a long blade, holding it out for Wilcox to see.

"Thanks, I'd rather not."

"Good."

George slipped the blade back in its sheath.

"Now, back to my question, who do you work for?"

"No one."

"Why should I believe you? How do I know that your compatriots aren't on their way here now?"

"No compatriots. By the way, if you're working on your American English, might want to stay away from using the word compatriot. Sounds like you Russians and your comrades nonsense."

"You think I'm Russian." George pulled the pack of cigarettes out again, offered them to Wilcox who shook his head no.

"You work with Boris."

"I see no harm in telling you that I am from Belarus."

"Interesting," said Wilcox. "You ski?"

"Yes."

"Well?"

"I went to the Olympics."

"Really. Good for you, George."

"It was a proud moment for my family. It led to my current position."

So not Russian. Belarussian. Same thing in Wilcox's mind, with a slight wrinkle.

"I never made it to the Olympics. I'll bet that was fun. Which one?"

George shook his head. "I've told you enough. Too much maybe. So, tell me, who was the man in the Range Rover? The one with the dog."

"That was a hobo I picked up in Alabama."

"He's a friend, no?"

"Sure."

"What kind of a friend?"

Wilcox knew this was coming. He'd wondered why Boris hadn't asked. Probably because he was waiting for George to show up and do the real questioning.

"Alright. He does missionary work here in the Philippines."

"So, he's undercover."

"Nope. Plain ol' run of the mill missionary. Spent time in the service but swore off guns. Good man. He doesn't know what I do."

George took a long drag from his cigarette. He held the smoke in for close to thirty seconds. When he spoke, he exhaled out of his nose. "A good story, Mickey. As believable as your cartoons. Why should I believe you?"

"Because Walt Disney would never lie to you."

A short cough of a laugh from George. He wiped his forehead with his pinky finger.

"Enough with the games. I played along. I let you down. Now, what do you say we get down to business. Tell me why you've targeted some very important Russians. And please tell me why I shouldn't just shoot you now."

A slim pistol slipped from George's pocket. What else did he carry on his person? Garrotes? Slipknots? A stray white rabbit?

"I told you. I work alone. Am I the first indie you've ever met in our line of work?"

"No. But most work for someone. I assume you do as well."

"Wrong. This is all me. Why is that so hard to believe?"

George shrugged. "What you do, killing, it takes talent, skill built from years of practice, experience. You Americans might call it 'grit'. You don't plot to kill without backing."

"I had backing. Not anymore."

"Tell me more."

"Not much to tell. My benefactor... how should I put it? I didn't need him anymore. I got my use and moved on."

"You killed him, this benefactor?"

"His name was Pluto the Dog, if you please."

"I'll take that as a yes. Ruthless. A pity you can't work for me."

"Not for a billion dollars, George. On second thought, you mind if I get another smoke? My head finally cleared."

George nodded, stepping forward, careful not to get too close. Not that Wilcox thought he could win that match again. Time. More time was what he needed.

Cigarette lit, a lungful of nicotine inhaled, Wilcox looked up at George.

"I don't fit the model of what you think you're up against, George."

The slim grin on George's face widened a notch. "Oh, do tell. I suspect some sort of high and mighty reason is coming."

"If by 'high and mighty' you mean 'killing every last dirty scumbag in the Russian government', then yeah."

George thought about this one, taking his time to reply.

"Why the Russians? Why not the Chinese?"

"Who says they're not on my list?"

"But you've—"

"Look, George, I don't care what you do to me. I really don't. I knew what I was getting into. Kill me. Torture me. Whatever. It's just me. No one else. I get a hard-on for killing communist pricks that are more interested in stuffing their fat pockets than taking care of their citizens. Nice adherence to the philosophy. Bet you never read Marx in your life. Maybe Groucho. You a Groucho fan, George?"

"An altruistic assassin. I don't believe it."

"I'm not altruistic, George. I'm just practical. Call me the modern-day garbage man. I don't give a shit about the actual trash. That's what you don't get. I get paid whenever I want. I kill whoever I want. No rules. Just do the kill and move on to the next. Like a kid at my buddy Walt's Disney World, I could do this twenty-four-seven. I live for it."

"You Americans and your false bravado. I'm not even Russian and I still see the hypocrisy."

Wilcox grinned. "Hypocrisy? What part of it?"

"You are a killer. What you do flies in the face of what you've just said. You're as bad as the men you've killed."

"Call it what you want, Georgie Boy. I take out the trash, plain and simple."

George dropped his cigarette to the floor, ground it out with his shoe.

"Very well, Mr. Mouse. We'll get what we can from you and then leave you for the dogs. It was... interesting to meet you. Enjoy your time with Boris."

George turned and headed for the door but paused before reaching for the handle. He looked back. "Oh, just one more thing."

"Shoot, Columbo."

"The boy, who was he to you?"

That hit Wilcox harder than he could've imagined. "You touch him and I'l—"

"You'll what? You're dead already."

"I swear—"

George held up his well-manicured hand. "Spare me. We'll find the boy. We'll find your friend in the Range Rover. They'll talk or they'll die. Simple as that. Enjoy the rest of your life, Mr. Mouse."

And with that, he opened the door and was gone.

Wilcox expected the goon squad to come right in. They didn't. Planning? Getting more tools? Or just giving him time to stew?

Matthew Wilcox sat on the ground, hands and feet bound, waiting for the pain to come. But all he could think about was what choice Cal had made: to stay and fight, or flee with Pindip to safety.

Either way Wilcox would die satisfied. He'd done his work and done it well. It was all in God's hands now, if Wilcox had believed in God.

As he sat there, he found himself hoping that there was a God, if not for himself, then for that little boy who deserved a better fate than him.

CHAPTER FORTY-FIVE

Soaked through and through, Cal trudged on, deeper into the gloom. Every once in a while, a strike of lightning would illuminate his way. Not that he needed it. He'd gone deep, purging the civilized and slipping into a different mode. He felt, rather than saw, everything around him. It was a sensation he'd often marveled at. The ability of a warrior to slip into something primal, ready to fight.

Liberty stepped lightly next to him. Not that anyone could've heard either of them if they stomped their way through the jungle. With the pounding rain and the booming thunder, a herd of water buffalo could've Macy's Day Paraded through here.

He passed the first grave marker minutes into his journey. Pindip's ghosts never materialized, but Cal did wonder if tsunamis or monsoons ever helped disgorge dead bodies from their final resting places.

They came to three pickup trucks a few minutes later. Empty. He put a hand on the hoods. All cold, but he couldn't tell if that was because of the rain or the fact that they'd been there a while.

He gave half a thought to waiting there, ambushing whoever

came back. Maybe they'd bring Wilcox out again. Or his lifeless body.

He spun in a circle, trying to see where to go next. There was no obvious path. No definite way further into the dark. He bent down and looked into Liberty's eyes.

"I need your help, girl. Can you help me find him?" Liberty cocked her head like she was trying to decipher his gibberish. "Help me find Matthew, girl."

She was no bloodhound. Would a dog with an overgrown sniffer even help in the downpour? Probably not. But Liberty had something, Cal could feel it. He'd felt it growing over the preceding weeks. That sixth, maybe even seventh sense.

Like Daniel, he thought.

Daniel and the others would be pissed that he hadn't waited. Inside he told himself that he was saving his friends from getting mixed up in Wilcox's mess. But was that really the truth? He'd called them, after all. Not the other way around.

Cal rustled Liberty's back. She didn't move, staring right through him.

"Let's find, Matthew, girl."

So, no sixth sense this time. Gotta do it the old-fashioned Native American tracker way. Or maybe just pick a way at random and go.

He went with option number two, hoping that he wasn't too late.

CHAPTER FORTY-SIX

The rest of The Jefferson Group made it to the airport, but not without a firm press against Manila's air traffic control. Every flight in was being diverted. They couldn't imagine why a small private plane would want to land in the worst storm of the year.

One of them had actually called the landing suicide.

The men in the back had their doubts, but when the brothers flying the plane grinned and called it just another day at work, what could they do but trust them. There was a fine line between bluster and reality. Ray and J.P. Connors had proven reality in the past. Go along for the ride.

A bumpy ride in and a skid-landing later, they deplaned, leaving the pilots to deal with the airport. They would've just taken off, but there wasn't anywhere they could go with the amount of fuel left in their tanks.

Luckily, their ride was waiting, courtesy of one of Gaucho's contacts. The nondescript SUV could've been a Mitsubishi or Subaru knockoff, and its paint job had seen better days, but when coaxed, the engine roared to life.

"See. I told you we'd be good," Gaucho said, already pulling away from the private terminal.

They made it to where the Range Rover was waiting. They'd had to backtrack no fewer than three times. This particular path was more than a little backwoods and the local cartography had more to be desired.

There was a light on inside the Range Rover. The first good news they'd had in hours. Neil had tried to contact Cal time and again. Nothing. Luckily, the GPS tracker he'd initiated worked in spurts. It showed the same spot over and over like a homing beacon.

"Take it slow," Daniel ordered, when the Range Rover was within walking distance.

Gaucho complied, slowing to a crawl, tires surged through the rushing water running through the back road.

The light in the Range Rover flickered, like someone's form had passed through the light.

Daniel unbuckled his seat belt. "Stop here. I'm going in on foot."

"I'm coming too," Top said, grasping the door handle.

A few ticks later, they were stalking closer. Again, the flicker in the cabin light. Something wrong about it. Daniel moved faster, hand tight on his weapon.

Top went to the passenger side while Daniel took the driver. Impossible for anyone inside to see them coming in the darkness. No way Cal was sitting inside a lit vehicle. All wrong.

The only thing there to greet him when he opened the door was the air freshener flapping back and forth in the wind, and a cell phone sitting on the driver's seat. No Cal. No Liberty. No kid.

Now what?

CHAPTER FORTY-SEVEN

Pindip shivered as he followed what he thought was the American's trail. He'd been to the ancient graveyard in the past. The ghosts had scared him and his companions away shortly after they completed their daring adventure.

There wasn't much to see on this go, and Pindip stutter-stepped every time something grabbed at his foot. The beetle-covered hands of ghouls reaching up through the mud to snatch him.

But he kept moving. He had to. Matthew was somewhere up ahead. He could feel it. Maybe the other American and his pretty dog had found him by now. But was he as skilled as Matthew? Had he taken out the Russians? No way to tell until he got there.

So Pindip did what he always did. He kept moving while ignoring the horror raging all around him.

There are no ghosts, he repeated to himself over and over again. And if there are...

"*Cross the streams!*" he said to the rain.

CHAPTER FORTY-EIGHT

Boris was all smiles when he came back into the room. This time it was just him, like he'd won the straw pull.

"We have fun now," the big Russian said, slapping his chest like a tribal warrior looking tough for the competition.

Wilcox exhaled. He could use another cigarette.

"Okay, Boris, like I told your friend from Belarus, I'm a little tired. Mind if I get a quick catnap before we start the fun and games?"

The words took time to process in Boris's mind. When he looked like he finally understood, he shook his head, his best impression of a sad proprietor. "No. We begin."

"Fine. Where do you want to start? Slapping? Or maybe spanking?"

The blade that slipped from Boris's waistband was all the answer needed.

"So, you don't think you can face off man to man?"

"I no be stupid."

"Coulda fooled me. Seemed like we've got all kinds of stupid going on around here. And not for nothing, pal, you're King of All Stupid. Tell me, when they recruit guys like you, do they give you a lobotomy before or after they give you your first dose of steroids?"

The lack of understanding was obvious on Boris's face.

"Did you register one word blowing across that wasteland between your ears, you drooling mesomorph?"

Instead of pressing for a translation, Boris actually raised the blade to his face and licked it.

"Classic," said Wilcox. "I've been thrown into a bad Rambo knockoff."

Boris pointed the blade at him, and then mocked slitting his own throat.

"Seriously? You need to get some new material. Tell you what, why don't you untie me, rent a plane, and I can take you to see some Girl Scouts. They'll show you how to act tough. They make great cookies too."

Boris's answer came in the form of a kick aimed at his prisoner's chest, like a soccer play punting the game ball downfield. It caught Wilcox perfectly, sending him flipping backwards. He took it, went with it, thanking his lucky stars.

The Russian followed the back flop, oblivious to anything but the kill. He didn't see Wilcox deftly slip his bound hand under his buttocks. Wilcox looked out to the world. Knocked cold with his face rising on his forearm, obscured by his half-curled body.

IT WAS ONLY natural that the American would be unconscious after such a blow. Boris had played rugby in his youth, a touch of football as a teen too. He was proud of his kick. Too proud.

So, he went for it again. The man from Belarus had said not to kill the American. That didn't mean he couldn't pummel the American to a pulp. It would be fun. Messy, but fun.

Boris stepped in with his left foot, a hop like he was midfield, his right foot cocked and already swinging in. He was careful to step to the side of the wetness on the ground. No sense slipping. That would be stupid, careless, all the things his father had told him not to be.

He could feel the impact, sense it before it came.

But it never came. He'd committed completely. The powerful sweep of his foot aimed at the American's head was well on its way when something incredible happened: the American moved, and not in the slow way of a man having barely regained consciousness. No, the American slid right, out of the way in the blink of an eye.

Overcommitted. That was Boris now. Slamming for the winning goal. He tried to arrest his momentum, his world slogging down to milliseconds. He felt his body rise as the sweeping kick took him onto his left toe. He really did try to stop, try to turn. What a cruel trick. Trying to arrest his momentum only made things worse. Instead of landing correctly, Boris's entire body twisted.

How slow could time go?

He was sliding sideways now, his once planted foot slipping under him.

And the American, what was he doing? Biting himself? Staring at Boris, biting his own forearm.

Alarm bells clanged in his head as Boris hit the ground, the knife held between he and the American for pathetic protection.

When the Russian crashed to the floor, the world still reeling in slow motion, Boris saw it. The thing between the American's teeth, the hands now in front of the smaller man's body.

Slow motion reared to full forward now, a mad scramble for life. It was only the second time in his time on Earth that Boris felt true fear. The first had been on an ill-planned mission in Afghanistan. He'd vowed never to go back and to never be under the ruling thumb of the Russian government.

But here it was again, that all-encompassing fear that made his body want to seize. He had to push through.

His right elbow hit the wood floor painfully, almost causing him to drop the knife.

Their eyes met. No fear in the American. Only straight determination. He watched as the man impossibly got to his knees.

Boris scrambled away, hot fear burning in all four limbs.

He tried to call out, but his contracted throat only let out a sort of grunting whine. He had to get to his feet. The razor blade in the American's teeth could do the job on the ropes that quickly.

Get to your feet! he screamed in his head.

He got as far as turning away from the American when bound hands looped over his head, quick as a cat.

Boris went to stab backwards, tried to roll back the way he'd come.

Then something touched the skin of his neck. Delicate, almost loving in its simplicity.

"Stop moving," the American whispered in his ear.

Boris froze.

"I like you, Boris. Don't make me draw this razor across your neck."

Boris almost nodded.

"Now, now. Wouldn't want my hand to slip. You had me up there for a while. Who knows what my weakened state might do to you."

As evidence, the tiny blade dug in, just a bit. Boris could barely feel it.

"Don't," Boris was able to say through his self-imposed *rigor mortis*.

"How many, Boris?"

"How many what?"

"Come on, Boris. We don't have time. How many men are outside?"

"Five."

"Including the Belarussian?"

No answer. He'd finally regained a measure of composure.

Wilcox tightened his grasp.

"I know what you're thinking." His words came in perfect Russian, like a true Muscovite. "You think you can overpower me. And as much as I'd like to see you try, don't. Now tell me, how many?"

"Six, including the outsider."

Wilcox thought that an interesting choice of words. But of course, a true Russian would look at a man from Belarus as an outsider, an imposter of Mother Russia.

"You have family, Boris?"

"No."

"That's a shame. I'm sure your grammy and mammy would be so proud of what you've become. Now, since my time is short..."

Boris only felt the pressure for the first moment, then came the pain. Again, he tried to call out. Not even a whimper this time. Wilcox had cut straight through. All that came out was a gush of deep red blood. Mouth opening and closing in a silent pantomime, Boris was let go, pushed away. He heard the American grab the knife from the floor. Boris's hands had dropped it as they moved to his throat to stem the flow of blood.

What a cruel trick. At least he would've liked to die in his home, in Russia. But here he was again, face to face with death in another armpit of the world.

He was able to flip over once and then again. He was too consumed with his own lifeblood to realize the American had let him go.

So, this was how it would end. The old fear of childhood flooded Boris's being, his body confused with despair. He was that tiny boy again, cowering and afraid of his father and his fist. He'd hidden for days, missed school, left his mother unprotected. Fear. Deep, freezing fear.

Then his vision cleared for a moment. Where was the American. Boris let go of his neck with one hand meaning to turn. He felt the warm gush against his now cold hands and clamped down once again.

There he was, that bastard American. He should be dead. Boris had wanted to kill him. Wasn't that why his superiors had sent him? To take care of the problem.

"You're a real piece of work, Boris," the American said. His Russian had a country flavor to it, like a man who'd spent his life in the fields. He turned Boris's own blade over and over in his hands. For some reason the thing fascinated Boris to the point of distraction. Vision going blurry then bright again. The sun. Had it somehow broken through?

Now his hearing, what was wrong with it? Going in and out, a short-wave radio out of tune, searching, never quite finding.

Boris's body rebelled then, sending him into a would-be coughing fit. Entire body convulsing, the blood gushed anew. He tried to stop it, tried to use all the strength he'd built up his entire life. After all, he was Boris.

And then he wasn't.

When his vision cleared this time, he saw the American clearly, standing over him, smiling. And then the blade plunging, a striking serpent, straight into Boris's chest cavity, past the ribs, through so much useless human tissue, and into his heart.

America and Russia locked eyes again, but it was Russia whose light was extinguished first.

CHAPTER FORTY-NINE

This is impossible, Cal thought, searching and never finding. The jungle seemed to go on and on. Without a map or some clue as to which way to go, he was going to get lost soon.

He stopped, tried to listen through the howling rain. Cal even knelt in the mud, Liberty huddled close against him.

The slam of a car door. The blast of a shotgun. Anything. Just a clue.

Nothing.

He was just rising to his feet when he felt Liberty tense. She was pointed the way they'd come, or was that the way they were headed? Easy to get turned around here.

No, it was the way they'd been walking.

Liberty pointed, not making a sound.

Cal followed her unwatered gaze.

One, two...

And then he saw it. So slight at first, just a hint of movement. It could've been the shadow of a swaying tree. But Cal waited, trusting his companion. And then the shadow moved again. Someone watching, tracking him.

He moved, and Liberty needed no prompting, although her attention was still fixated on the now stationary shadow.

He crept from tree to tree.

He felt nothing, not the rain, not the sliver of cold cutting through his clothing. He only saw. And as he moved farther around in a wide loop, he saw clearer, until finally he was in perfect position.

CHAPTER FIFTY

For some reason, Pindip wasn't scared. He'd been through all manner of storms, and darkness was his friend. He embraced anything that could hide him, as only a child of stubborn strength could.

He'd caught glimpses of the American and the dog. He was more concerned for the dog. He'd seen firsthand the uncanny ability of animals. How did a beast of burden know when a human snuck into a barn to get some much-needed rest? How did a rooster know exactly when to make its early morning call? How did fish know to swim in schools?

He'd often wondered of these things, the treasures of nature was how he thought of them. Animals. Plants. Things he could see but couldn't quite understand.

And so it was with the American's dog, Liberty. Pindip felt that she understood the situation better than any of the human in this God-forsaken place. That's what the priest had called this place: God-forsaken.

It sounded terrible. A place of monsters.

He pressed on despite his fear – a child not yet a man doing something that adults four times his age would never do.

He absorbed every shadow, every movement through his reptilian brain. He calculated distances without thinking, sorted plant from plant, threat from no threat. At one point, he'd seen the vague outline of a trio of feral hogs scuttling by. He wondered if the American had seen them.

And now here he was. He was close. He'd never been to the complex, but he'd heard the stories. Stories of evil men willing to do evil things.

God-forsaken.

A snap of a branch. Then another.

Frozen in place, he honed in on the sound's location. Loud enough to be heard over the storm. Not a tiny twig but a hefty branch. A coincidence? A trick of the night?

No. Man-made.

Seconds ticked. He waited.

Then he saw it, the movement. Then the light. Faint at first and then wavering back and forth. People.

He counted two and then two more. Who were they? Friends of the American?

His curiosity dragged him forward, toward the light.

CHAPTER FIFTY-ONE

George yawned into his hand. He'd sent Boris's charges to the vehicles. The idiots hadn't even brought supplies with them. If they were to get what they could from the brave, if stupid, American bound in the other room, they'd need more water and food. Interrogation took time, and George felt like his was slipping away. His superiors wanted answers. He wanted answers.

This man who insisted he be called Mickey Mouse, of all things, was a cagey character, a worthy opponent.

He reflected upon his decision to confess that bit of personal truth about his youth training for the Olympics. Early years were a source of pride both for himself and his family. He could still see the look on his father's face, the puff of pride that had come when he'd been told that his oldest son had made the team. He would represent Belarus. He would be the shining example of all that was good after the oppressive stranglehold of the Soviet Union.

He'd made the trip to that faraway land, his first outside the country. It had been an eye-opening experience. But not for the reasons he'd told his parents. Of course, he'd enjoyed the Western food and women. He was an elite athlete after all, one of the best in the world.

But as unlikely as it had seemed at the time, he'd been most entranced by the silent minority touring the crowds. The Russian spies who'd approached him on his second night abroad. Only the man and woman weren't Russians, not technically. They were from Belarus.

There were never names given. George still marveled at the way they'd found him, courted him, and then lain the hook. It had been so simple, yet so effective. He'd slept with the woman that night. Despite being ten years his senior, or so he thought, she was passionate in bed. She let him have control.

That's not to say that sex ensnared George. No. It was something more. If ever asked, and no one did, he'd probably say it was merely one of the more pleasant perks of the job. Not a prize. Never that. Being a spy is a lonely business, and letting another human being in on your secret opens up a certain level of intimacy, an intimacy that often turned to lovemaking between consenting adults.

He'd won silver at the Olympics. Gold had been just within reach, but his competitor, a Russian (from Moscow, of all places!) cruised to victory on what would later be deemed a tainted run juiced by performance-enhancing drugs.

He should've been happy to take the gold that was rightly his. But he didn't. On those days that he could be himself, he went to his hidden apartment and pulled out the worn box and stared at his silver medal. It was his reminder that the world wasn't fair, that the competition would cheat to win. George never forgot that. While an honorable profession to a point, spying left ample opportunity to cheat and be cheated.

He thought of his first love now. In his mind, he called her Natalia. Such a beautiful name, a movie star name. And she had been beautiful and cunning. She and her partner, an equally gregarious man whose name he also could not recall but didn't bother to name in his memory, trained George, gave him the right to become a spy for Russia. It paid well, and some years they met in far off accommodations to celebrate wins, trade stories, or just be who'd they'd been born to be: human.

And now there was this man, this American. So brash. So determined. So fierce yet... ah what was the word? His Natalia had it. The ability to flip an attitude like a switch. A chameleon in human skin. Deadly and daring.

Ah, Natalia, how you would have liked this American.

He himself liked the American very much. He'd watched the man take Boris, literally head-on. Any warrior worth his weight could do that, but it was the look in the man's eyes, that something you couldn't manufacture, and George had tried over the years. Pain and suffering, usually stemming from hard childhood, wasn't something you could duplicate in training. That hardness, that callous look on life, was something the Universe injected into your soul in tiny increments over time until you were fully immunized.

George had it. Natalia had it. And the American had it.

Maybe I shouldn't kill you, George thought, lighting another cigarette. He really hated the habit. He'd technically quit years ago. It didn't really go with being an elite athlete, but something about smoking and spying went together like Russians and corruption. That made him laugh. Ah, the Russians. How they thought they owned the world. Take his handlers for example. They thought they held the strings of his life.

Oh, how sadly mistaken they were.

George played both marionette and puppeteer. The Russians didn't need to know that. They'd been good to him. All except for that idiot from Minsk. He'd been a delightful kill. All that pent-up animosity made George's job quite satisfying when the grease finally flew off the frying pan. Beware to any who stood nearby.

George finished half his cigarette and threw it off the high porch, into the cascading rain.

Maybe he would buy a place on this island. He didn't mind the heat or the bugs. He didn't even mind the storms. It seemed fitting. Like home.

He took one last look out into the darkness, exhaled, and went back inside to take care of the American.

CHAPTER FIFTY-TWO

It had taken Wilcox the longest minute of his life to cut through all his rope bonds. Killing Boris had been mostly about adrenaline, that beautiful juice that had gotten him through all manner of jams.

But now his limbs shook. Even the knife he held wavered along with his vision. He had to get out fast. The window would be best.

The first he'd tried was hammered shut. As was the second. Last chance was the only door – the portal to the rest of his enemies. *Shit.*

No time like the present, Matty boy.

He didn't so much creep as hustle his way to the door. He never made it. He did, however, have time to plaster himself against the wall when the door swung open.

George strolled into the room like it was a walk-in closet. Wilcox saw him pause, letting his eyes adjust to the gloom.

Move, Wilcox told himself.

Blade ready. Body surging once again with dregs of adrenaline, Wilcox lunged. But there was to be no surprise. Despite his appearance, and his languid performance from before, George was quick, squirrel-quick, in turning away from Wilcox's move.

The deft shift – an Olympian's agility – put the American off-balance and his feet slipped. He almost fell. If he had, there was no doubt that George would've been all over him. As it was, the man from Belarus didn't make a move. Sure, he gave his rival space. Sure, he pulled out his pistol. But he didn't shoot. He only smiled.

"I thought that lump on the floor was too big to be you," George said, motioning to the dead Boris. "Poor Boris. He was as loyal as an old dog. He had no, what do you call it, personality? But he was invincible, or so I thought."

"I'm not that easy to kill."

"Impressive." George thought on his comment and then amended. "Maybe not as impressive. You'd agree?"

"Don't over-eulogize him. He was an idiot, a gorilla in spy's clothing."

George chuckled, not lowering his weapon a millimeter.

"What should we do, my American friend?"

"Oh, so we're friends now?"

Wilcox had to do something soon. The trickle of emergency juice wasn't keeping up with demand.

"Whatever gave you the impression that we weren't friends?"

"I don't know. Maybe it was the fact that you sent Boris in here to kill me."

George looked disappointed, even sad. "I did nothing of the sort. I told our now-deceased sadist to soften you up. Wouldn't you have done the same?"

"I don't order others to do what I can do just fine."

"A fair jab, though... never mind. Back to my original question: what should I do with you?"

Wilcox was trying to get a read on the man. This was his thing, his best talent. He'd used it to get what he wanted whether from his deadbeat mother or his absentee father. Mindreading was a lost art.

"I'll go back to what I said earlier: Let's fight it out, one weakened spy against another."

"I assume you are the weakened one. I feel fine. Fit as a fiddle."

God, the man sounded like an American. Wilcox wondered how many Georges roamed the blessed hills of America, posing as normal citizens, spying for their Mother Russia.

"Then let's duke it out. Come on. Mano a mano."

"I think not."

"You don't think you can take me."

"American bravado again. So tiresome."

Thunder shook the humble building. Rain hammered against the wooden enclosure, Mother Nature doing her best to beat her way in.

"Come on, George. Let's do it. Let the best man win."

George actually seemed to be considering it. A wondrous thing, pride. You jab just enough and you get anyone riled up. George looked like a poker player weighing his odds on the next hand. Up the ante or stay put?

"Very well."

George placed his weapon on the ground. It was all Wilcox could do not to lunge for it. But he'd promised George a fair fight, if there was such a thing.

"Show me what you've got, Georgie."

The first sign of trouble came when George took off his suit coat and then started unbuttoning his dress shirt. It was impossible to miss the muscle tone. The man who had seconds before looked like a billion workers slaving the days away in a muggy high rise, now turned into something different. The disguise slipped. Underneath it was the Olympian

"You really should think about this, you know. I'm all for fair play, but you, well, you should look in the mirror."

"What? I feel great." Wilcox stretched his shoulders, cracked his neck back and forth, biting back the pain of every movement.

George chuckled. "You Americans and your bravado." He was shirtless now, pants coming off like a karate champ getting ready for another lazy day on the mats. There wasn't a shred of fat on the man, and he moved with elegance, a complete ease that made Wilcox feel like he was looking in the mirror.

Down to boxer briefs now, George motioned for Wilcox to step to the center of the room. The American did so, noting the way George tracked him, like a hunting cat.

They squared off, two champions gauging their respective chances.

Time for the fight of my life, Wilcox thought.

George nodded, jaw clenched. The signal for the fight to begin.

Wilcox moved first, a sweeping kick aimed at his opponent's legs. Even as his foot reached out, it felt he was moving through syrup.

His opponent had no problem hopping over the move.

"Too easy," George said, bobbing left and right, stretching as he went.

"Don't flatter yourself. I'm just getting warmed up."

George nodded. No fear there. Merely an attitude somewhere on the spectrum between tolerance and boredom. This was this man's life, or so it seemed.

Wilcox struck again, this time with his fist. A left and right jab to judge the Belarussian's distance. George was only too happy to show him, dancing just outside his opponents reach.

"You're slow," George said.

"Like I said, just warming—"

Wilcox barely saw the strike coming. It was a glint of movement. The strike smashed into the side of his face, spinning him around. His world swam and he almost fell to his knees.

He tried to shake it off, tried to get his bearings. The Olympian denied him the chance, wading in, face set, fists loose and fully in control. The barrage began and he was now Wilcox the punching bag. All he could do was wrap himself the best he could, waiting for a lull, an opening, anything.

Those things never came.

On and on the beating went.

Wilcox was on his knees, his breath coming in sharp heaves.

His left arm hung useless at his side. He was sure a handful of ribs were broken.

Then, all at once, it stopped.

Wilcox chanced a look up. George was looking down at him, his chest rising and falling in a steady rhythm from the workout. "It's a shame. I would've like to have done this on your best day."

Wilcox tried to get the words out, but a glob of blood filled his mouth. He spit it out, tried to stand.

"Don't bother."

The fist came down hard, untouchable, impossible to block.

Wilcox took the blow and saw the edges closing in. He saw his own blood on the floor as he lay there. Then the iris closed, the black swallowing him whole.

CHAPTER FIFTY-THREE

Pindip watched the lights dance back and forth. It wasn't the Americans. It was the same Russians who'd taken him. They didn't seem to be too concerned. Pindip followed them for a moment, even considered distracting them in some way.

From what he could figure, they were going back to the vehicles.

There wasn't time to find out. He had to keep moving. Matthew must be wherever the Russians had just come from.

He took a careful step forward, still watching the lights fade away. Another step, ankle deep in mud that sucked his foot down.

A hand came down on his shoulder, and the boy screamed.

CHAPTER FIFTY-FOUR

Daniel's ears perked up at the scream. It was hard to calculate its distance. The rain was too thick, the ambient noise turned up to a roar.

Gaucho came up then, searching.

"Where do you think that came from?"

Daniel pointed. "That way."

"Okay. I think we should split up. You wanna go toward the scream or take the long way around?"

"The long way," Daniel said.

"You think that was the kid?"

"Probably."

"Right, well we better get moving."

No more words were needed. They'd already known that Cal was in trouble. It was like a warning signal in the air. The scream only lent the signal more credibility.

The only thing Daniel was worried about was getting there in time.

CHAPTER FIFTY-FIVE

C al and Liberty heard the scream. Before Cal had time to think, the dog was off, running away from her master and towards the anguished cry.

Cal started after her then stopped. He was torn. Two ways to go.

Had the Russians found Pindip? Or was it Daniel and the others? Why the scream? The scream sounded too close to be coming from the Range Rover. Maybe another kid.

That was impossible. What kid in their right mind would be out in this storm? It had to be Pindip.

No time to think. He followed Liberty, at least for twenty feet, and then something else got his attention, another sound. He strained to hear. What was it? The storm?

No. A helicopter.

CHAPTER FIFTY-SIX

Pindip's all-consuming scream had him locked, facing the intruder who had him latched by the arm. The boy screamed and screamed until a finger came up from somewhere beneath the folds of darkness. The finger pushed back the cowl just enough for Pindip to get a glimpse of the interloper.

It was the old man, the witch doctor, the shaman, the man the villagers said could look into your soul, pull it out, tie it in evil knots and shove it back in like sawdust into a stuffed bird. It was the man from the hut who'd helped Cal and him find where Matthew was.

He touched a finger to his lips. Pindip's scream caught in his throat.

What was the man doing here? He'd lured them there. That had to be it. He'd told them to come to this cursed place where ghosts and their kin gathered. Maybe they needed a sacrifice. Pindip's mind jumped to the stories of the older boys at the church's makeshift orphanage.

He breath grated in his chest.

"They are coming," said the ancient man.

It took Pindip a moment to sort through the words. They

sounded no more tangible than a whisper on the wind, a breeze against the might of the storm raging all around them.

"Who's coming?"

"The Russians."

The finger pointed again, this time back the way Pindip had been walking. That's when the boy saw it, the flashlight. They were coming his way.

Pindip made to run. The man could take care of himself. But he, Pindip, had to get away, find his path to Matthew.

But the hand shot out again and pinned the boy in the place. There was the silent finger again, now pointing to the left.

"Hide."

"Where?"

The man took deliberate hold of Pindip's rain-sopped shirt and dragged the boy along until Pindip could propel himself. He had to trust the smelly shaman. It was his only hope.

CHAPTER FIFTY-SEVEN

The Russians had heard the scream like everyone else. They remembered the boy. Who else would be insane enough to not only be out in the monsoon, but to be in this accursed place? More than one of their number had begun mumbling some long-remembered prayer to whatever god was listening when they heard the scream.

"That way," the self-proclaimed leader said. Without Boris, he was in charge. But with these men, being in charge was a momentary responsibility, not a right. Hard men lived by hard rules, and Boris was the only one strong enough to rule them all.

"We should go to the cars," another man said.

"Yes. The supplies."

The sub-leader coughed out a derisive laugh. "Cowards. Come. Boris will kill us if he finds out the child is here. Let's take care of it."

And so, they trudged onward. All it took was the mention of their cruel leader's name to get them moving. There'd been more than one severe beating in the past for more minor infractions.

Weapons at the ready, they followed the path of the scream.

They were close. They could feel it. They'd been close to the vehicles, but there would be time for that.

The leader, whose name was Misha, forced one foot in front of another. His proclamation moments earlier had been little more than bluster. He held two secret fears. One was an inflated fear of the dead. His mother had been as superstitious as Stalin had been a murderer. She'd filled young Misha with images of horrible spirits and ghostly ghouls roaming the earth. He had seen all manner of atrocity, some at his own hand, and he'd always gotten the feeling that he was creeping closer and closer to that final confrontation with his dead mother's spirits.

But it wasn't a ghost that swooped down or a skeleton that reached up from the muck that came to call. It was the suppressed round from an American-made weapon, one well cared for and lovingly carried by a warrior whose shot would not miss. The final calling card of Misha's life came in the form of a bullet scorching through his throat, then another through his brain. Misha didn't have time to think about ghosts, he just had time to lay down and die.

CHAPTER FIFTY-EIGHT

Daniel's first two shots took down the lead man. It took his comrades about five seconds to respond. The sniper could see why. The way the man went down could've been mistaken for a fall. Two of the dead man's companions even bent down to help the corpse up. No deal.

Instinct kicked in from there for the men. One man's fire set off a domino effect. They fired in all directions, none of their rounds coming close to hitting Daniel.

And so, Daniel did what he'd been trained to do, what he did now without a thought. He took out another, and then made his way closer.

He needed to take at least one man alive.

CHAPTER FIFTY-NINE

Gaucho and Top watched as the first man went down. The short Hispanic chuckled to himself when the other bent down to help the dead man.

Gaucho shook his head with shame for the man. "Stupid."

"But still armed," Top replied.

The ensuing barrage of gunfire raked the tree line, though the storm did a fair job of dampening the sound.

"It's really coming down," Top said, conversationally.

"Sure wish I'd brought an umbrella."

"I've got one back in the car. Want me to get it for you?"

"Nah," Gaucho replied. "Wouldn't want you to go to the trouble."

"You sure? It's got little duckies on it."

Gaucho flipped the bird at the Master Sergeant. Top grinned in return. Friends to the end.

But this was not to be their end.

They waited until someone had assumed control over the group again. When Gaucho looked around the tree this time, there were only three men standing, weapons and flashlights still scanning all around.

"Stupid," he said again.

"Let's go. I don't want Briggs to have all the fun."

"Yeah. And my underwear's soaked through. Cal better reimburse me for my boots too."

Another grin passed between the best friends, and then they broke from cover and descended on the survivors.

CHAPTER SIXTY

Too many options.

Cal had heard the helicopter and then the gunfire. He only hoped it wasn't the kid. Not much he could do about that now. Surely Daniel and the others were there by now. He'd have to leave Pindip's safety to them.

He followed the sound of the helicopter amidst the roar of the storm. A couple minutes later he made it to a two-story structure that sat up on stilts.

Cal thought he saw one and then another guard tower in the distance, illuminated by nasty strikes of lightning. Lightning and thunder were trading insults with one another; one scorching in followed by the crashing answer of the other. It wasn't unlike the feeling of being under a mortar or artillery barrage.

There was only one way up to the main level of the structure - a single ladder.

He lost the sound of the helicopter. Maybe it was just a play on his ears. How the hell could anyone be flying in this soup?

He made it to the ladder without incident.

Good. Careful now.

The ladder was at least two stories long.

He shoved the pistol in his waistband, took a deep breath, and started climbing one slippery rung after another.

The thought was not lost on Cal that any halfwit with a gun could probably shoot him right now.

CHAPTER SIXTY-ONE

Four out of five Russians were dead or dying. The last would be joining their partners soon, whose blood mingled with the torrents flooding the ground.

The last man on his feet, Pavel, had dropped his weapon. Impossible not to. He was surrounded by three men who'd dispatched his comrades in record time.

He'd seen slaughter like this before, but at his own hand. Those had been innocent women and children waiting to be taken to a refugee camp. Boris didn't believe in refugee camps. He said they were a breeding ground for terrorists. And so, the last man standing had shot them without a thought.

Funny how he thought about that now. His past sins. He'd known they were there. But at barely twenty-three years of age, life was judged not by the dead, but by the living.

Three men facing him. He could just make out their faces. The short one, the one with the strange beard, he looked more dwarfish than human. The type he often battled online in his pretend world of reality.

The second man, a huge man, tall. His skin shone in the darkness, its deep ebony competing with the darkness for superiority. And the man was clearly winning.

Then there was the third. There was something about this one. Any normal man or woman, maybe even a child, would have thought the man with the blond hair and ponytail the least threatening. But the surety in the man's gaze sent tendrils of warning through the Russian's body. The man with the blond hair was a killer, the kind they wrote about in his favorite comic books. Like Captain America and the Winter Soldier. No, not the Winter Soldier. For some reason the Russian's mind searched for the Winter Soldier's name, the one he'd had before being captured by the evil Hydra. Buddy? Billy? No, Bucky!

The jubilation was short-lived.

"Where are they?" the blond man asked. He spoke in English. American English. Good. Then maybe he had a chance.

The Russian shook his head. At this, the large black man marched over, grabbed him by the front of his shirt and lifted.

"Talk to my friend," the black man said.

Pavel searched for the right words. Of course, he knew English. You had to know English to buy a beer in London or a hamburger in Hawaii. Ah Hawaii. How he'd loved the place. His mind often wandered like this, in new and inconsequential tangents. In this case, it had more to do with the drugs coursing through his system - drugs Boris didn't know the rest of them had. The big man forbade the taking of drugs on missions.

The black man shook him.

"Hey, I said, talk."

"Yes," the Russian stammered. "I... he..."

"Maybe he doesn't know English," the dwarf said.

"Oh, he knows English," the black man said, his eyes never leaving his prey.

"Yes. I know English," said Pavel. "I know."

Desperation now. He felt the walls closing in. Paranoia

seeping in at the end of his high? Or was it just the situation? He wasn't particularly scared, and outside his current chemical state he might've seen what was wrong with that. Fear told the body what it should and should not do. Fear was natural. The mix of cocaine and high-end meth had him buzzing on an ethereal plane well above fear. But the paranoia...

"Where are the rest of your friends?" The black man gave him a shake.

"Here." The Russians eyes shifted to the ground.

"Not these, the others. The big man and the one you took. Where are they?"

Pavel was about to answer when everything changed. Some sound, familiar to him yet foreign to their current environment. Was it...? Yes, a helicopter. But it couldn't be, could it? Not in this mess.

The others heard it too, including the black man who eased the Russian to the ground.

"That can't be what I think it is," the shortest American said, scanning for the sound. It had disappeared, melted into the din of the storm.

If Pavel could only reach behind his back. Yes, slowly now. The rain would mask his move. Slowly now...

His hand grasped the hilt of the blade, the one he'd picked up in Pakistan. A wicked thing, something you could gut a pig with in one slice. He'd seen a man impaled by the blade. Not by him, but by Boris. It had been his first mission and Boris had given him the blade, slick with blood, as a gift for a successful first fight.

Yes, the blade. Amphetamine strength and determination flooded the Russian. He could do it. He would kill the black American, take his weapon and then kill the others. They were distracted, still searching for the mysterious helicopter. Not that it could land here. The canopy was too thick.

The blade slipped out. So easy. So fine. He could taste the bite of edge on skin, cutting deep like a master butcher. He even got as far as having it by his side, a model prisoner not doing anything wrong. Wait for it. Wait.

The sound of the helicopter returned. The black man pivoted just enough, just far enough that Pavel saw his opening. Quick now.

His aim was dead accurate.

But the aim of Daniel Briggs was truer, surer, a weapon in an expert's hand. None of that shoot the hand business. No. Too close to his friend. Too dark for an accurate shot.

Two rounds sliced into Pavel's body, sending jolts of pain coursing through him like a flood tide. He still held the blade in his hand. Everyone had turned now.

A new sensation slipped through his body, not the welcome high of the shipment they'd stolen from the Filipinos. No, this was something darker, blacker than the night, blacker than the skin of the American he was now looking up at.

"Dumb move," the black man said.

And he was right. Pavel didn't feel the blade slip from his hand. He didn't feel himself fall to his knees.

The second shot had done its job the best, nicking the dying Russian's heart. As the marked man's life slipped away, all he could think about was where he'd gone wrong, and why death felt so empty.

CHAPTER SIXTY-TWO

Liberty streaked through the darkness. She saw everything. Her finely tuned senses felt the presence of more friends. Friends from home. Friends of her master.

She passed them by. She had to. Something else pulled her on. The scream of the boy. The boy from the car.

Yes. On she ran, cutting a blaze through the storm. She honed in on the mark in her brain.

She heard gunshots. The master? He could take care of himself. The master always did.

But the boy...

On she ran, her wolf brain determination focused, so that an explosion in her path might not have deterred her journey.

A scent in the wet air. A scent among myriad scents. The boy.

Run.

Run.

Close now.

Run.

She caught a glimpse of the fading shadow nearby. Too big to be the boy. But there he was.

Sorting through the jumble, the dog made a wide loop, the

better to take in the view. She'd learned that a straight path might not always be best. It would take longer, and the cunning that cut through her rebelled against millennia of breeding. The straight shot was the way of her race. Straight and true. The wolf breaking from the pack to kill the deer. Food for a week.

But this was no food. This was far from food. This was life. A child's life.

How did she know? She didn't care. One thought usurped all others in her primordial brain: Protect the boy.

The night blurred around her. Onward.

Then their eyes met. The boy saw her, even reached out a hand.

Liberty turned in earnest.

The man walking with the boy, he saw her too.

Deep set, evil eyes. Not the obvious disdain for life of so many humans, but the basest evil of an animal, a mortal enemy.

Liberty snarled deep inside. She almost howled.

Almost.

CHAPTER SIXTY-THREE

D ragged by the shaman, Pindip saw the streak in the darkness, thought it was a trick of his vision. When he looked closer, he recognized her, Cal's dog.

Liberty, his mind called.

He saw her eyes flash, the lightning illuminating her path.

But where was the American? Why was the dog not with him?

That was when Pindip's body seized, rooted him to the stop.

The shaman took another step forward before noticing that his charge had stopped. He hadn't seen the dog yet.

"Come, boy."

When the man turned this time, there was a leer in his eyes. The boy recognized it for what it was, as it lay in the pit of men's souls. Some had control over it, while others allowed it to possess them. It was a soiled thing. Something terrible.

Godforsaken.

"Leave me alone," Pindip said, backing away.

"What is wrong with you, boy? I'm taking you away from this place."

"No."

All cunning and pretense left the man's features. In the garish

light of lightning, his intent was clear now. Pindip never should
have gone to the hut. He'd heard the stories, but he'd ignored
them. He thought things would be different with the American.
He thought the veil of fear would be lifted, and for a time it had
been.

But now here he was, staring at the visage of a demon. The
thing stretched one arm out wide, the other tucked beneath his
robes.

"Come, boy. Do you want me to take you to your American?"

That almost convinced Pindip. Maybe he was wrong. Maybe
the situation, the storm, the night, maybe it was all jumbling his
senses. It had happened only once before, when he'd been so
hungry that he could barely tell night from day.

"No." The word floated from boy to man.

The knife came out, gleaming and well-worn. Its curved blade
matched the wicked smile of the man.

"You'll come with me, boy."

"No."

Pindip backed away. Another step. *You'll have to run.*

The man stepped closer.

Pindip had been able to ignore the smell before, the smell that
had rocked Cal back on his heels. But it wafted off the man now
like the exhaust from hell.

"Do as I say."

Pindip didn't answer. There was no time. He had to get away.
He had to run. But why did it feel like the man would catch him
without a thought? He'd snuck up in the darkness, the ever-astute
and wary Pindip caught completely unaware.

The only warning the two got was the low growl that might've
been the bending of trees branches nearby. Only it wasn't. It was
the arrow blazing in, fifty pounds of fury.

The shaman had just enough time to turn and face his future.

Liberty pounced, her aim true.

The shaman staggered back with the weight of the dog, her impact compounded by wolfen rage. He tried to protect himself, even attempted a pitiful slash with his blade, but it was not to be.

Terrible, croaking screams came from the demon. And then there was silence. And the hideous open eyes of an evil man fading away.

Pindip stepped closer. Took the blade from the man's hand. There was still life in him.

He'd never killed a man, but the man would die soon. Liberty would see to that. Her eyes met Pindip's and there was under-standing there ‑ the same understanding of his angel, of his Matthew.

The blade struck next to where Liberty's mouth had been. It was impossible to distinguish the blood from the muck covering the man, but the spasm that racked the man's body was all Pindip needed to know that his aim had been perfect.

He pulled the dog away and there they stood, boy and beast, watching the last thrashings of a monster. When he was sure the man was dead, Pindip stroked Liberty's head. She whined.

"Come," the boy said, and together they ran off into the darkness.

CHAPTER SIXTY-FOUR

Matthew Wilcox came to in a blink. No subtle slip back into reality. This was more like an electric jolt.

"Welcome back," said a voice.

He bit his lip to stave off the pain. "You still here, George?" he managed to squeak out.

"Still here."

The Belarusian's form appeared. Wilcox's vision came to, slower than the rest of his senses. How hard had that blow been? By the pounding in his head he rated it a nine on a scale from one to holy cow.

"I'm confused. Why am I not dead yet?"

"I don't know."

"Come on, George," he rasped. "You always have all the answers."

Thunder rocked the room.

"I tell you, I'm not sure."

"Look, if you're not going to kill me, could you at least get me a drink of water?"

"Sit up."

Wilcox tried but he found that his body, mainly his cramping legs, wouldn't comply.

"Give me a hand?"

"I'm not that stupid."

It took a few excruciating moments for Wilcox to right himself. Ribs. Legs. Head. How bad? No way to know. Everything was source of pain.

"Can I have my water now?"

George handed him an unopened bottle. Even that was hard to handle. He felt like a baby trying to open a food jar. He finally got it opened and didn't mind chugging the delicious liquid down. When he was done, he looked up at George. His body was only barely lined in blur.

"So, you wanna tell me what the hell is going on?"

George took a deep breath and said, "A possible change of plans."

"I knew it."

"Oh?"

"You like me. You really like me. I knew we'd hit it off. Come on, George, tell me where we're going. The Bahamas? How about Tahiti. I haven't been there in ages. You can wear your little speedo with the flag of Belarus on the ass end and I can go diving for lobster. Whatdya say? You like lobster, George?"

George lit a cigarette and blew the first drag into Wilcox's face. "Where do you get your sense of humor?"

"There's a joke factory in Sweden. I sent them fifty krona and they sent me a sense of humor. Refurbished, of course."

"You speak like the people in your ridiculous American movies."

"I thought we'd been through this, George. I have mommy and daddy issues. Great movies and smut TV raised me. Hell, ask me about any of the Housewives of Orange County and I can give you the lowdown."

"Housewives of..." George must have realized he was getting pulled in, because he cut himself off. "As I said, there's been a change of plans. We're leaving as soon as the storm lets up."

Wilcox motioned to the ceiling. That simple movement send spikes of pain coursing through both his pecs and his biceps.

"Doesn't sound like the rain's stopping anytime soon, George. Maybe you should take a load off. Join me on this ever-comfortable floor. Hey, you know if they shot the movie Rambo in this joint? Seems like it. I'll bet they strung up Sly Stallone right over there."

No response from George. Either he was bored or preoccupied. Wilcox couldn't tell. Wilcox couldn't tell a lot of things, like whether he'd ever pee standing up again or if his eyes would be crossed the next time he looked in the mirror. All he knew was that he was in a world of hurt, and that the only thing keeping him from wincing in pain was jabbering on like a wiseacre.

"Come on, George. Tell me what's going on. I promise I'll shut up if you tell me."

"Why don't I believe you?"

"Because you think I'm a swell guy, and one swell guy would never tell another swell guy to shut his mouth."

Now George smiled. "Joke as much as you want. Pretty soon you won't have much to joke about."

"What is it? Is Boris's younger brother coming by? How do you think he'll feel when he sees Boris rotting on the other side of the room? Speaking of rotting, is that smell him or did you let one rip?"

George looked away. Something had caught his attention. Wilcox had to strain through the ringing in his ears to hear much more than the pounding of rain. Then he heard it. There it was, faint, but growing louder.

How the hell had someone gotten a helicopter through this shitstorm?

Wilcox felt his departure chances slipping away like sand through a sieve.

CHAPTER SIXTY-FIVE

Cal was close to the landing when he heard the roar of the helicopters engine. He even saw the red-light glow from the open door.

He kept climbing. He scuttled over the final lip and rolled over and over, staying as low-profile as he could, fully expecting the rounds to come cutting in at any moment.

They didn't. The helicopter disappeared again. Cal didn't have a second to think on why. This was his chance. He took it.

The door was cracked open. No sign of life so far. If Wilcox wasn't inside, well, then he was shit out of luck.

But out of luck for what? Why was he even here?

What the hell are you doing?

He shut the question down, the master tamping down the impetuous apprentice.

Slipping inside, weapon leveled, he scanned the interior. All he found were piles of discarded water bottles and the remnants of MREs. He had the faint memory of a particularly disheveled staff sergeant in Guam. The man had been court-martialed for filth.

Still, not a soul, just the mess.

There was another door through what appeared to be an ante-room of the place.

This was it. It had to be. Wilcox was in there. Cal could feel it.

He slunk off to one side of the room, always watching the dim glow of light from under the door ahead. When the door opened, he crouched down in the shadows.

A man emerged.

He was just stripped down to his boxer briefs. With his spotless, trim physique, he looked as vanilla as a scoop of America's finest ice cream.

The man had a pistol in his hand. That much Cal could see.

The man went to the door Cal had entered through and disappeared.

Something wasn't right here.

He pressed on while watching for the stranger to return.

The next door was closed. The knob was little more than a rustic block of wood. Cal gave it a twist. It turned with a screech and he pushed open the door.

His eyes went long first, to the pile on the other side of the room. A body.

I'm too late.

Cal was about to walk that way when a voice croaked from somewhere in the corner to his left.

"You back already, George?"

Cal stalked the sound, finger pressed on the trigger.

"Listen," said the voice, "if you didn't get pepperoni on that pizza, you take it right back and tell them who's boss, understand?"

There was no mistaking it. The voice belonged to a broken body. The wiseassery belonged to Wilcox.

Cal said the name. No answer at first. Then a short cough of a laugh and, "Hey buddy, I knew you'd come for me."

Cal hurried now. As his eyes adjusted to the just-illuminated room, courtesy of a Coleman lantern in the opposite corner, he saw the man curled just feet away.

"Wilcox? Are you okay?"

"Depends on what you mean by okay."

Wilcox shifted and Cal saw the rope binding his hands to his ankles.

"Who was the guy that just left?" Cal asked, handing Wilcox the knife from his pocket.

"Please tell me you killed him."

"No. Who was he?"

Wilcox sawed faster. Cal saw his entire body shake with the effort.

"Here. Let me help you."

"No," Wilcox snapped. "Watch the door."

Cal did, and counted down as Wilcox cut through his bonds. It was close to a minute before he was finished. The man who'd effectively kidnapped Cal stretched his wrists.

"God, that hurts."

"Can you walk out of here?"

"Does the Pope snack on mozzarella?" Wilcox handed the knife back to Cal.

Cal helped him up. The man was weak, even feeble. Wilcox couldn't take Cal's weapon if he tried.

Wilcox was draped over Cal's left shoulder, a pistol in the Marine's right hand. Not ideal, but he'd have to make do. There was the whole other issue of the ladder when they got there.

"Let's get you out of here."

And they almost did. They made it to the exterior door when it burst open.

And Daniel Briggs stepped inside.

CHAPTER SIXTY-SIX

"Cal. Are you okay?"

"I'm fine." Cal motioned with his head to Wilcox. "He's the one who needs help."

"Who, me? I feel right as rain."

Daniel didn't move, not even when the form of MSgt Trent stepped up behind him.

"Hey, Cal, what are—"

Cal cut him off. "The guy who just left. Where is he?"

"What guy?" Top asked.

Cal cursed himself for not shooting the man when he'd had the chance, or at least hogtying him until he had a chance to ask questions.

It was Gaucho who cut off further discussion. "We need to get off of this thing," he said when he appeared behind Daniel. "Oh, hey, Cal."

"What is it?" Daniel asked.

"The helo, I think it's letting guys off right back there. I can't be sure. I couldn't see that far."

That got everyone moving. No telling how many men were on

the bird. Best not to be sitting in a teetering building when they arrived.

They made it down the ladder, Wilcox the only one to struggle, although he didn't complain.

Once on the ground, Cal took charge.

"We go deeper, see if we can skirt..."

That's when he saw it, the first form coming into view. The others were already peering into the darkness, weapons trained. Not an ounce of fear, just steel determination.

And so it was with complete surprise when a familiar voice called out, "Cal, it's Todd Dunn. We've come to help."

CHAPTER SIXTY-SEVEN

Cal was embarrassed to feel the relief shoot though his body. Todd Dunn had taken over Cal's father's company, SSI – Stokes Security International, after Marjorie Haines, the company's former CEO, had left to become the president's chief of staff.

"Dunn?"

There were more forms now, fanning out. Their men. Their friends.

The former Army Ranger came forward slowly. His weapon was pointed at the ground as he approached.

"Do you have Wilcox?" Dunn asked. Straight to business. Much like Daniel, there was rarely extended conversation with the man. He was just one of those solidly dependable soldiers who stood as resolute at the Great Wall of China.

So why did Cal hesitate? Why didn't he want to tell Dunn that Wilcox was here?

It was the doubt. The doubt that Wilcox had planted about Cal's friend, the President of the United States, Brandon Zimmer.

"We've got him."

Cal could make out Dunn's features now, hard and a perfect match to his no-nonsense attitude. But there was a relaxation in response to Cal's affirmation that Wilcox was in custody. He even felt the rest of Dunn's team relax, edges loosened, nerves allayed.

"We can take it from here," Dunn said.

"Thanks, but I think we can handle it."

Dunn was adamant. "Our friend wants him in custody, now."

"He *is* in custody."

The friends stared at each other. The only thing that broke the tension was the bark that came from somewhere off to the right.

Heads and weapons swiveled in its direction.

"Don't shoot!" Cal yelled over the storm. He wasn't sure the troops would listen. Technically they were his men. Or were they? He wasn't CEO of his father's company. He'd been released from that burden. And now, standing in the pouring rain, watching as Liberty and the Filipino boy emerged, he couldn't help feeling that he had zero control over the current situation. These men weren't his men, they were Dunn's men. They were the president's men. Both were his friends.

Then why did it feel like he was facing the firing squad?

Pindip took his time. Then he saw Wilcox and he ran.

Cal put up a hand for everyone to stay calm.

Wilcox wrapped the boy in a silent, sobbing hug.

Liberty was back at Cal's side, and the dog seemed to feel exactly the same as its master: unsettled.

"We have orders to bring Wilcox in," Dunn said. Now that Pindip had pinpointed the international assassin, the weapons had been raised again.

"I said I can handle it." Cal said over the roar of the monsoon.

Dunn stepped closer. Cal knew that look. It wasn't for a handshake. The hammer was about to fall.

"This isn't up for discussion, Cal."

The Ranger stood mere feet from the Marine. This was a conversation for the two.

"And I said I can handle it."

Dunn didn't grit his teeth, didn't adjust his features with the complication. Not his style. He went back to rote, to his orders. The good soldier. The president's man.

"I'm taking Wilcox out of here. You're welcome to come along."

Daniel, Top, and Gaucho were by Cal's side now.

"Hey, Dunn. How they hangin'?" Top asked.

No answer from Dunn. Not even an acknowledgement of his friend's question.

"Whoever flew that bird in here was one badass dude," Gaucho remarked.

Still nothing from Dunn.

Cal felt his closest friends shift, the imperceptible move of anticipation.

All except Daniel, who stood there, unmoving, like he already knew how the movie would end.

"How about an escort to our vehicles?" Cal asked, trying to lighten the situation.

Dunn went back to the company line. "Mr. Wilcox is to be taken into custody and returned to the United States."

"Yeah, I know. He's under my custody and I'm going to take him home."

"If it's all the same to you guys," said Wilcox, "I sure could use a working bathroom and a meal."

"Shut up," Cal growled.

"Fine, but it was up to me, I'd get us the hell out of here before the rest of the Russians show up."

Dunn looked at the man. "What rest of the Russians?"

Wilcox laughed. "The guy you just let slip by you, he's from Belarus, but he works for Mother Russia. I'd say right about now he's watching us from somewhere out there," he pointed to the darkness beyond the hasty perimeter. "He's just waiting for his friends to show up. Now, if you don't mind, I sure would like an ice-cold glass of milk and a big ol' slice of apple pie."

Dunn glared at the man, the mask of calm finally shifted.

"Look, Dunn," said Cal, "let's get out of here and I can talk to our mutual friend. There are things to discuss."

Dunn's gaze shifted from Wilcox to Cal. That's when Cal felt the cold shudder run the length of his body.

"You're not getting it, Cal, you're not in charge here."

"What's that supposed to mean?"

"It means that you've been AWOL for weeks."

"You can't be serious."

Dunn's face said it all. Cal's finger crept back to the trigger of his weapon. No one saw it.

"I wasn't going to say this here, out of respect for our... friendship, but my orders are clear."

"And what are your orders, Dunn?"

"I'm here to take you all into custody."

"Under whose authority?"

"You know exactly whose authority. Now, we don't need to make a scene. I'm sure we can get it all settled once we get home."

Something clicked way down in Cal. Everything came together. Everything Wilcox had said. Everything he'd seen. Everything he'd been thinking.

Zimmer was now part of the problem. He'd been sucked up by the system.

The pistol came up, not pointing directly at Dunn, but just in the right position that everyone got the point.

"Hey boys, why don't we go somewhere more comfortable to talk about this," Top said.

"Yeah, no need..." Gaucho tried to interject.

It was Daniel who took another step forward. For everything Cal couldn't say, that small movement said it all. Even Dunn felt it.

"Leave it be, Dunn," Daniel said.

Cal bristled at the thought of his best friend embroiled in what was clearly his own personal mess. But the die had been cast.

Troops in jungle camouflage moved in closer, the noose tightening.

"Give him to me," Dunn said.

"No." Cal turned to Wilcox. "Go."

Wilcox flashed the shit-eating grin that Cal had become so accustomed to.

When Cal turned back to Dunn, he faced the business end of the man's weapon.

"Do not move," Dunn said in calm, measured tones.

"What are you going to do, shoot me?"

"I don't want to."

Die cast.

Cal's pistol came up, and Daniel raised his as well.

It was obvious by the look in Dunn's face that this was far from what he'd expected. *No shit, Sherlock.*

"Come on, kid," Wilcox said to Pindip.

Cal saw them walk away from the corner of his eye.

Dunn didn't move. Didn't even look Wilcox's way.

"See you around, Stokes," Wilcox said. "It's been a real..." He scratched his head. "Shit, I didn't think I'd ever have a loss for words."

"Just go," Cal replied, still not completely understanding what he'd just done.

Wilcox laughed. "Later, buddy."

Over the rain and pounding thunder Cal thought he heard Wilcox say to the young boy, "Did I ever tell you about the time I spent with the Cirque du Soleil as a trapeze repairman?"

SOMEWHERE OUT OF EARSHOT, the man from Belarus watched it all by virtue of hidden camera, and listened by virtue of a directional mic. He watched the heated confrontation. He watched man and boy walk away. With his camera, which took pictures in multiple spectrums, he got it all.

And finally, he had a name: *Stokes*.

The man from Belarus wondered where that man might lead.

He waited until the entire troop departed, and then he extracted himself from his hiding space, and made his way out of the jungle, untouched and unseen. Just the way he liked it.

CHAPTER SIXTY-EIGHT

Msgt Trent had convinced Dunn, after a long standoff, to let them leave on their own accord.

The questions on the way home had been short, answered with barely a curt nod from Cal.

Daniel watched it all, trusting his friend, but concerned for where Cal's decision had taken them. Daniel Briggs had lived through all manner of danger. It kept him wary but didn't deter his course. What did make him pause now was the same thing that kept Top and Gaucho whispering to themselves: How would the president take the news?

There'd been no calls, no request to divert from their path home. Nothing. Two days passed, then three. Still no call.

And then, one lazy Saturday in Charlottesville, as The Jefferson Group enjoyed a round of coffee on the back porch, a familiar face appeared.

The President of the United States, Brandon Zimmer, friend to everyone gathered, their boss, passed through the sliding doors from the kitchen leading out to the backyard.

It was the first time Daniel had really noticed how much the man had aged. He was still the same man, just weathered, like the side of a barn, his temples were going to gray and deep-set cuts of black accentuated the areas under his eyes. He was a harder man now, a president who'd seen his fair share of adversity. Zimmer often called it the rude awakening of the first world. The rest of humanity knew the evils of man, but America still had the naive intention of youth. A couple months in the Oval Office had a way of opening a man's eyes to reality.

Everyone – except Cal – rose when Zimmer stepped onto the porch.

"Good morning, gentlemen."

It was Top who marched forward and stuck his hand out.

"What can the pride of the Marine Corps do for our commander-in-chief?"

On another day, Top might've picked the president up in a bear hug, or at least offered a polite slap on the back. Not today. Tension stood on end, soldiers pointing their pikes in all directions.

"Hey, Top," Zimmer said warmly.

"Can I get you a cup of coffee? Guatemalan Antigua, French-pressed."

"I'm already three in, but thanks." Zimmer looked around at his friends, Daniel, Gaucho, Neil, Doc Higgins, and finally Cal. "Can you guys give me a minute?"

The message was clear.

"No problem," Top said. He waved his hand for the others to follow him inside.

Daniel tried to share a final look with Cal, but his friend's glare was locked on the president.

Not good.

"YOU LOOK NO WORSE FOR WEAR," Zimmer said, walking over to Cal.

"I'm fine."

"That's not what Dunn tells me."

"I'm fine."

Long pause. Cal had been waiting for this little tête-à-tête.

"And our friend Wilcox?"

"Gone."

"Yeah, I heard."

"So, why are you here?"

"Can't the President of the United States come to town to see his old friend? I wanted to make sure the stalwart Cal Stokes is okay."

"I said I'm fine."

Zimmer was visibly shaken by Cal's curtness. He took a seat, unbuttoning his suit coat. "Place looks nice. New landscaping?"

"Cut the crap, Brandon. Why are you here? Is Dunn inside, handcuffs waiting?"

The two friends glared at each other for a long moment. Zimmer's eyes softened first.

"What happened in the Philippines... it shouldn't have happened like that."

"So, is this an apology tour?"

"I didn't say that."

"Well, maybe you should apologize."

Zimmer swiveled in his chair to get a better look at Cal. "What happened to you? Weeks without word and the next thing I know, you let the very guy go who blackmailed you. Not just you. You and your friends."

Cal took a deliberate breath in.

"I thought they were your friends too, or are we expendable now?"

"What the hell is that supposed to mean?"

Cal fought the urge to shoot out of his chair.

"It means you're one of them now. You bought into all the bullshit."

True confusion on the president's face. "I don't know what you're talking about, and if you think acting like a petulant child is going to—"

"I'm the one acting like a child? How about the way you're dealing with foreign affairs? Is that the way an American president should act? I thought we were fighting for something. I thought we were trying to get things done."

"We are."

Cal shook his head. "The way I see it, you'd rather pander to North Korea, let them off when they're dodging sanctions on a daily basis. Do you know what they're doing to their own people? Do you know the havoc they're planning to spread all over the world?"

"Of course I do," Zimmer snapped. "What do you think it is I do all day? Not all of us have the luxury of taking month-long vacations, you know."

Both men were breathing heavily now. Zimmer seemed to be fighting the urge to avoid eye contact.

"Look," said the president, "Let's start over. I'm here to see you, to make sure you're okay. The thing with Wilcox... we can deal with it."

Cal couldn't relax. He didn't know if he could ever relax again. "This isn't working."

"Fine. Take a day. Hell, take seven. Come see me and we'll get it all worked out."

Zimmer rose. The resolution was clear in his head.

"No. I don't mean Wilcox, I mean this. You and me. The Jefferson Group's relationship with the White House."

Zimmer's face hardened. Gone was the old friend. Here was

the leader of the free world. "Take some time," he repeated, slow and even. "You look like you need it."

Cal jumped out of his chair.

"We made a deal, dammit."

"What are you talking about?"

"When we first started, we agreed that politics, international treaties, that none of it would get in the way of doing the right thing. You're going back on your word."

Zimmer's eyes narrowed, cat-like.

"What do you want me to do, Cal? Send you overseas so you can kill every red-blooded killer out there?"

"I don't see anything wrong with that."

"Well I do, dammit! I'm the President of the United States of America, for God's sake. I can't—"

"But you have. You *have* ordered us to kill. What changed, Brandon?" Cal was regaining his composure now.

"I have a country to think of. Hell, I have the world to think of. What do you think would happen if the President of Russia found out that you let his ambassador's killer go?"

"I'll take care of him myself."

Zimmer's eyes went wide. "You're crazy, you know that? I was trying to be nice before. The rest of them – even Marge thinks you should be committed. If the CIA or the FBI knew, you'd be in jail right now."

Cal held out his hands, wrists together. "Then take me. If that's what you think is right."

Neither man spoke for what seemed like a very long time.

The president exhaled and looked down at the ground. He looked tired, beaten literally and figuratively. "I'm not taking you in. You know that." He took his seat again, avoiding Cal's eyes.

"We can still do this," Cal said. "You weren't the only one that went soft. I did it too. But, and I can't believe I'm saying this, Wilcox showed me the way. There's so much more we could be doing. I can hit the road right now, start recruiting while Neil and the rest of the guys start tracking down every scumbag from here to Mars." He walked up to his friend who was still looking away. "We can do it. Just like before."

After a moment, Zimmer looked up, his eyes tinged with sadness. "I can't."

"Why not?"

"I told you." Zimmer's back straightened. He got up from his chair and adjusted his tie. "I'm the President of the United States. I won't order you to come with me, but I will order you to stand down."

"Or what?"

Zimmer was incredulous now. "You don't want to go there, Cal."

"We're already there. Tell me what happens if I go off on my own."

Zimmer shook his head. "I'll have no choice."

"To do what?"

The president looked deep into his friend's eyes. "I'll send them after you. With everything we've got."

The ultimatum hung in the air like a spinning scythe.

"Okay. Then I guess we've come to it."

"You can't be serious. Cal, if you—"

"Yeah, you already told me. And don't worry, I won't ask the others to come with me. But I won't stop them from coming."

"You're cut off. No help. Not even a phone call."

Now Cal shook his head, the die cast flipped him to the next page. The notice stamped and stuffed in the mail. "Probably best that way."

"Cal—"

Cal put up a hand. "It's okay. You warned me. I get it."

They stood there for a long time. Neither man knew quite what to say.

Finally, Zimmer stuck out his hand. "For what it's worth, I wish I could go with you."

"Then do it. Come with us."

"I'm the president, I can't just—"

"It's been done before," Cal said with a smile. Of course it had been done before. That's how Zimmer had become president in the first place.

"Forty eight hours to settle your affairs. After that..."

"I understand."

The two men shook hands like friends, then hugged liked brothers.

"Don't do anything stupid while I'm gone," Cal said.

Zimmer gave one final nod before making his way back to the sliding door. He was just reaching for the handle when he seemed to remember something and turned back. But he just stared for a moment, and then continued on his way, the president once again.

THE MEN of The Jefferson Group had come to the realization that their fellowship was at a temporary end.

"So that settles it. Daniel and I are off in a day, maybe two. Top and Gaucho..."

"Yeah, yeah, we know," Gaucho said, seeming completely unconcerned by what had just transpired. "We'll see you when we see you."

"Don't' worry, Cal. I'll keep our little buddy out of trouble," Top said, wrapping an arm around his best friend, who squirmed to get out of the larger man's grasp.

Cal ignored the feigned struggle and addressed the others. "Doc, you stick with Jonas. I don't think they'll bother you as long as you stick to what we're actually supposed to be doing around here."

"It'll be quiet around here without you," Jonas Layton, the CEO of The Jefferson Group said. The concern he'd voiced earlier was etched clearly in his tone.

"Nonsense. I think some peace and quiet is just what the doctor ordered," Dr. Alvin Higgins said, taking a sip from his gin and soda. "I've been meaning to catch up on some reading, and maybe I'll finally get back to my research. Imagine that."

Cal could only smile. Higgins had faith that they would be back. Cal wasn't so sure. From everything he'd learned on the road with Wilcox, from all that had been said between he and the president, his future was anything but clear.

But as he looked around the room at his friends, at the men who'd put their lives on the line for him time and again, he hoped that they would all be back together one day. One day soon, hopefully.

At least they had one more night to toast to their friendship. And then it was just he and Daniel, two souls on the road to find some truth in the world. What was that truth, and how long would it take to find? It would be up to fate to decide.

So be it, Cal thought, as he grabbed another beer from the ample supply in cooler, and went back to enjoying the precious last moments with his friends.

I hope you enjoyed this story.
If you did, please take a moment to write a review on Amazon. Even the short ones help!

Want to stay in the loop?
Sign Up to be the FIRST to learn about new releases.
Plus get newsletter only bonus content for FREE.
Visit cg-cooper.com for details.

A portion of all profits from the sale of my novels goes to fund OPERATION C4, our nonprofit initiative serving young military officers. For more information visit OperationC4.com.

ALSO BY C. G. COOPER

The Daniel Briggs Novels:

Adrift

Fallen

Broken

Tested

The Tom Greer Novels

A Life Worth Taking

Blood of My Kin

Stand Alone Novels

To Live

The Warden's Son

The Interrogators

Higgins

The Patriot Protocol Series:

The Patriot Protocol

The Chronicles of Benjamin Dragon:

Benjamin Dragon – Awakening

Benjamin Dragon – Legacy

Benjamin Dragon - Genesis

ABOUT THE AUTHOR

C. G. Cooper is the USA TODAY and AMAZON BESTSELLING author of the CORPS JUSTICE novels, several spinoffs and a growing number of stand-alone novels.

One of his novels, CHAIN OF COMMAND, won the 2020 James Webb Award presented by the Marine Heritage Foundation for its portrayal of the United States Marine Corps in fiction. Cooper doesn't chase awards, but this one was special.

Cooper grew up in a Navy family and traveled from one Naval base to another as he fed his love of books and a fledgling desire to write.

Upon graduating from the University of Virginia with a degree in Foreign Affairs, Cooper was commissioned in the United States

Marine Corps and went on to serve six years as an infantry officer. C. G. Cooper's final Marine duty station was in Nashville, Tennessee, where he fell in love with the laid-back lifestyle of Music City.

His first published novel, BACK TO WAR, came out of a need to link back to his time in the Marine Corps. That novel, written as a side project, spawned many follow-on novels, several exciting spinoffs, and catapulted Cooper's career.

Cooper lives just south of Nashville with his wife, three children, and their German shorthaired pointer, Liberty, who's become a popular character in the Corps Justice novels.

When he's not writing or hosting his podcast, Books In 30, Cooper spends time with his family, does his best to improve his golf handicap, and loves to shed light on the ongoing fight of everyday heroes.

Cooper loves hearing from readers and responds to every email personally.
To connect with C. G. Cooper visit
www.cg-cooper.com